STORY TELLING SEVENTEEN

I0537511

STORY TELLING

Unique & Different

STORY TELLING SEVENTEEN

A DIFFERENT SLANT ON LIFE

ISBN 978 1 9164697 7 8

Published by

Percychatteybooks Publisher

© Percy W Chattey 2019

Percy W. Chattey has inserted his right under the Copyright, Designs and Patents Act, 1988, to be identified as the author of this work.

Featuring
Famous Names
of the Past

This month we look at

Robinson Crusoe

&

H.G.Wells

As told by Richard Seal

STORY TELLING SEVENTEEN

Percychatteybooks is self-regulating to the contents and reserves the right to alter, change or edit articles and is not responsible for any advice given or knowledge that is imparted and recommendation, guidance or information should be checked on independently before acting on it.

All the individual work in Story Telling is published with full authority of the originator. If the reader needs further information concerning one of our 'Story Tellers' then please send an email to percybooks@outlook.com we will pass your request on to them

Story Telling Seventeen

As always, my gratitude to my lovely wife Jean, friend and soul mate, who has helped with the editing and all rewrites, also listening to all my ramblings whilst putting these articles together.

My appreciation to the following
In no specific order

Derek Cook for the cover
Richard Seal
Terry Tumbler
Sarah Dawkins RN, BSc (Hons) MSc <u>AMC</u>
Trudie Oakley
Higher Perspective
Allan Holdgate
Robert A Hall
Roald Dahl
Graham Strachan
and Meg

 *My name is Meg, and as in the past I will be your host throughout this creation. But first let me explain the following as it is very important:*

The contents and the opinions shown or written here are not necessarily the views of 'Story Telling' or its publisher and are published as articles of interest and amusement only and no offence of any kind religious, racial or political is intended to any person or group of people.

I would also like to add on behalf of Story Telling, in a world where there is so many fake and dishonest stories being bandied around, we cannot guarantee items printed here as being accurate or correct and they should be checked in other ways before acting on them.

 *Let's make a start with this label on a childs clothing and remember it is best to always read the label*

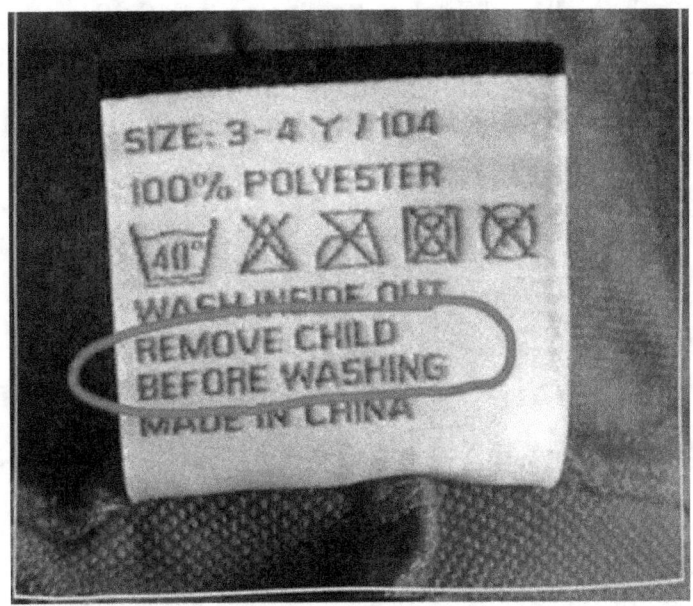

**

Story Telling Seventeen

 *Have you heard* about the little old ladies, Connie & Evelyn were sitting on a park bench outside the local town hall where a flower show was in progress. The short one, Connie, leaned over and said, 'Life is so boring. We never have any fun anymore. For $10.00 I'd take my clothes off and streak through that stupid, boring flower show!'

'You're on!' said Evelyn, holding up a $10.00 bill. So Connie slowly fumbled her way out of her clothes and, completely naked, streaked (as fast as an old lady can) through the front door of the flower show.

Waiting outside, her friend soon heard a huge commotion inside the hall, followed by loud applause and shrill whistling. Finally, the smiling Connie came through the exit door surrounded by a cheering, clapping crowd.

'What happened?' asked Evelyn.

'I won $1,000 as 1st prize for 'Best Dried Arrangement..!'

**

Quotation from Hitler

"He alone who gains the youth, gains the future,"

Story Telling Seventeen

LITTLE JOHNNY IS BACK:

The teacher asked the class to use the word "fascinate" in a sentence.

Molly put up her hand and said, "My family went to my granddad's farm, and we all saw his pet sheep. It was fascinating."

The teacher said, "That was good, but I wanted you to use the word 'fascinate,' not 'fascinating'."

Sally raised her hand. She said, "My family went to see Rock City and I was fascinated."

The teacher said, "Well, that was good Sally, but I wanted you to use the word 'fascinate'."

Little Johnny raised his hand, but the teacher hesitated because she had been burned by Little Johnny before. She finally decided there was no way he could damage the word "fascinate," so she called on him.

Johnny said, "My aunt Carolyn has a sweater with ten buttons, but her tits are so big she can only fasten eight!"

The teacher sat down and cried.

**

Quotation from Hitler
"Who says I am not under the special protection of God?"

Happy Couple

Richard Seal

Nick feels so weary seeing his eyes looking so bloodshot and bleary after a long stag night in the pub. He often wonders how he could tell his mates that he does not really like drinking beer, talking about women, football, or fast cars. The man often grits his teeth, seething through a smirk, grieving for precious time not spent with like-minded types over a coffee, discussing books, watching films, and taking turns to be the friend who cooks.

Planned for weeks by her friends, the Hen Night's arrival filled Cathy with a deep- seated sinking dismay. A few quiet drinks had descended quickly into hitting vodka hard, tequila slammers, and falling in and out of nightclubs. Adjusting her fixed grin, she had suffered in silence amid all the whoops and hilarity, whilst adorned by a red L-Plate. She would have much preferred to curl up on the sofa, listen to some classical music and sip tea over feline chat.

How much had the happy couple drunk last night? The bar staff were not keeping count or judging customers on the amount they consumed, as long as they kept it down and avoided starting a fight. Nobody had noticed a girl sitting quietly crying, or cared about the man being sick in the car park. They kept the tills ringing. Those in service kept calm, professional, offering everyone a winning smile and all the ladies ice and a slice.

The groom stands still, staring straight ahead, trying not to shake in dark suited sobriety. His mouth is getting dryer while his pale face is soaked and white shirt darkening with sweat. The bride's big day started with a cold compress, some weak tea, and soluble pain solutions. The couple swallow hard, so green queasy in front of rows of smiling faces. Feeling tender, second hand and breaking wind in front of the vicar was not what had been planned.

Computer Problems

A woman customer called the Canon help desk with a problem with her printer.

Tech support: Are you running it under windows?

Customer: 'No, my desk is next to the door, but that is a good point. The man sitting in the cubicle next to me is under a window, and his printer is working fine.'

The Keyboard

Tech support: 'Okay John, let's press the control and escape keys at the same time. That brings up a task list in the middle of the screen. Now type the letter 'P' to bring up the Program Manager.'

Customer: I don't have a P.

Tech support: On your keyboard, John.

Customer: What do you mean?

Tech support: 'P'... on your keyboard, John.

Customer: I'M NOT GOING TO DO THAT!

I'm Fine

A farmer named Paddy had a car accident. He was hit by a truck owned by the Eversweet Company. In court, the Eversweet Company's hot-shot solicitor was questioning Paddy.

'Didn't you say to the police at the scene of the accident, 'I'm fine?' asked the solicitor. Paddy responded: 'Well, I'll tell you what happened. I'd just loaded my fav'rit cow, Bessie, into da... '

'I didn't ask for any details', the solicitor interrupted. 'Just answer the question. Did you not say, at the scene of the accident, 'I'm fine!'?'

Paddy said, 'Well, I'd just got Bessie into da trailer and I was drivin' down da road...'

The solicitor interrupted again and said, 'Your Honour, I am trying to establish the fact that, at the scene of the accident, this man told the police on the scene that he was fine. Now several weeks after the accident, he is trying to sue my client. I believe he is a fraud. Please tell him to simply answer the question. '

By this time, the Judge was fairly interested in Paddy's answer and said to the solicitor: 'I'd like to hear what he has to say about his favourite cow, Bessie'.

Paddy thanked the Judge and proceeded. 'Well as I was saying, I had just loaded Bessie, my fav'rit cow, into de trailer and was drivin' her down de road when this huge Eversweet truck and trailer came tundering tru a stop sign and hit me trailer right in da side. I was trown into one ditch and Bessie was trown into da udder. By Jaysus I was hurt, very bad like, and didn't want to move. However, I could hear old Bessie moanin' and groanin'. I knew she was in terrible pain just by her groans.

Shortly after da accident, a policeman on a motorbike turned up. He could hear Bessie moanin' and groanin' too, so he went over to her. After he looked at her, and saw her condition, he took out his gun and shot her between the eyes.

Den da policeman came across de road, gun still in hand, looked at me, and said, 'How are you feelin'?'

'Now wot da foock would you say?
**

An Answer to a Teacher:

So what if I don't know the meaning of the word 'apocalypse'? It's not the end of the world.

A wise person once said:

1. We all love to spend money buying new clothes but we never realize that the best moments in life are enjoyed without clothes.

2. Having a cold drink on a hot day with a few friends is nice, but having a hot friend on a cold night after a few drinks - Priceless.

3. Arguing over a girl's bust size is like choosing between Molson, Heineken, Carlsberg, & Budweiser. Men may state their preferences, but will grab whatever is available.

4. On average, an American man under 75 will have sex two to three times a week, whereas a Japanese man the same age will have sex only one or two times a year. This is very upsetting news to most of my friends, as they had no idea they were Japanese

**

Special Travel Package for Businessmen

An Airline introduced a special package for Business men. Buy your ticket, get your wife's ticket free!

After great success, the company sent letters to all the wives asking how the trip was.

72% of them gave the same reply..."What trip?"

Helpmates

Richard Seal

Jean and Janet have spent all their lives taking every chance to help each other: At school, their homework was shared, knowledge and ideas pooled; calm words were always spoken if one of them was scared; boyfriend advice was freely dispensed, often with a hug; decisions were discussed; and any favour never needed to be asked for twice. As they went on to become wives and mothers, each woman became a special aunt to the children of the other. While the passing years have inevitably taken their toll, the elderly ladies embrace their roles as mutual helpmates. Nothing is too much trouble: joy for one is happiness doubled.

For these two soul mates, walking together and talking to each other was always such fun; Strolling through the decades at a leisurely pace, never dreaming of running; so happy sunning themselves while shooting the breeze, taking their ease, preferring to chew the fat about their beloved families and dear dogs and cats. Finally, their legs have given out, but neither of them really cares about that because it has given them a new interest to share. Jean loves to show off her range of ornate steel-capped canes, while Janet cannot wait to demonstrate her new 'bells and whistles' wheelchair, top of the range.

Every Wednesday the ladies continue to sit happily sipping milky coffee in their favourite corner cafe, which has survived somehow albeit greatly changed since their youth. They say little to each other; both smile slightly as a middle-aged waitress bustles past their table, walking comically fast, and the busy sounds of different generations' background chitter chatter natter drift past. Just one look with a hint of a wink and a familiar furtive grin, a cheeky playfulness within, is all it takes to reflect the fun, warmth, happiness and love - comforting and undemanding - between the best of friends of more than sixty years standing.

**

TOMORROW:
One of the greatest labour saving devices of today ??

"The books transported her into new worlds and introduced her to amazing people who lived exciting lives. She went on olden-day sailing ships with Joseph Conrad. She went to Africa with Ernest Hemingway and to India with Rudyard Kipling. She travelled all over the world while sitting in her little room in an English village."

Matilda by Roald Dahl,

✳✳

The Lady and the Bed

EVER SINCE I WAS A CHILD, I'VE ALWAYS HAD A FEAR OF SOMEONE UNDER MY BED AT NIGHT. SO I WENT TO A SHRINK AND TOLD HIM: "I'VE GOT PROBLEMS. EVERY TIME I GO TO BED I THINK THERE'S SOMEBODY UNDER IT. I'M SCARED. I THINK I'M GOING CRAZY."

"JUST PUT YOURSELF IN MY HANDS FOR ONE YEAR," SAID THE SHRINK. "COME TALK TO ME THREE TIMES A WEEK AND WE SHOULD BE ABLE TO GET RID OF THOSE FEARS."

"HOW MUCH DO YOU CHARGE?"

"ONE HUNDRED FIFTY DOLLARS PER VISIT," REPLIED THE DOCTOR.

"I'LL SLEEP ON IT," I SAID.

SIX MONTHS LATER THE DOCTOR MET ME ON THE STREET. "WHY DIDN'T YOU COME TO SEE ME ABOUT THOSE FEARS YOU WERE HAVING?" HE ASKED.

"WELL, $150 A VISIT, THREE TIMES A WEEK FOR A YEAR, IS $23,400.00. A BARTENDER CURED ME FOR $10.00.

I WAS SO HAPPY TO HAVE SAVED ALL THAT MONEY THAT I WENT AND BOUGHT A NEW PICKUP TRUCK."

"IS THAT SO?" WITH A BIT OF AN ATTITUDE HE SAID, "AND HOW, MAY I ASK, DID A BARTENDER CURE YOU?"

"HE TOLD ME TO CUT THE LEGS OFF THE BED. AIN'T NOBODY UNDER THERE NOW."

IT'S ALWAYS BETTER TO GET A SECOND OPINION

Robinson Crusoe

By Richard Seal

" ... fear of danger is ten thousand times more terrifying than danger itself." -
Daniel Defoe, Robinson Crusoe

'Robinson Crusoe', first published in London in 1719, was Daniel Defoe's first long work of fiction. It has been widely hailed as the very first novel, and the book introduced two of the most-enduring characters in English literature: Robinson Crusoe and Friday.

Crusoe himself is the narrator. He describes how, as a young man, he ignored his family's advice and left his middle-class home in England to go to sea. When he sails for Africa he is captured by pirates and sold into slavery. He escapes to Brazil, where he acquires a plantation and prospers. Having made a deal to sail to Guinea, buy slaves, and return with them, Robinson's ship is hit by a storm in the Caribbean. He is the only survivor, washed up onto a desolate shore. The castaway salvages what he can from the wreck and ekes out an existence on the island that consists of spiritual reflection and practical measures to survive. He documents all his experiences in a journal.

After many years, Crusoe discovers a human footprint, and he eventually encounters a group of native people who bring captives to the island to kill and eat them. One of them manages to escape, Robinson shoots his pursuers and the man is keen to serve his Master, the man who saved him. In time, he turns "my Man Friday" into an English-speaking Christian. After almost three decades the castaway departs (with Friday and a group of pirates) for England. He settles there for a time after selling his plantation, but eventually returns to the island and learns what happened after the Spanish took control of it.

It seems likely that Defoe's novel was based in part on the real-life experiences of Alexander Selkirk, a Scottish sailor who requested to be put ashore on an uninhabited island in 1704 after quarrelling with his captain, and stayed there until 1709. However, the author enhanced his work with a distinctive narrative voice, through which we share the castaway's experiences and reflections. Aspects of travel literature and adventure stories are also included, which boosted the novel's popularity. It is not only a compelling tale, but also a reflection on power, ambition, self-reliance, society and civilisation.

'Robinson Crusoe' was a popular success in Britain, and it went through multiple editions in the months following its publication. By the end of the 19th century, no book in English literary history had enjoyed more editions, spin-offs and translations, with more than 700 alternative versions. The story remains popular, through a range of television and movie adaptations, and was recently revived in the Tom Hanks film, 'Castaway' (2000).

"It is never too late to be wise." -
Daniel Defoe, Robinson Crusoe

The Machine

A young executive was leaving the office late one evening when he found the Chairman standing in front of a shredder with a piece of paper in his hand.

"Listen" said the Chairman. "This is a very sensitive and important document and my secretary has gone for the night. Can you make this thing work for me?"

"Certainly" said the young executive. He turned the machine on, inserted the paper and pressed the start button.

"Excellent excellent" said the chairman, as the paper disappeared inside the machine "I just need 1 copy" !!!!!!!!!!

**

"Have a heart that never hardens, and a temper that never tires, and a touch that never hurts." — Charles Dickens

Story Telling Seventeen

Standing the test of time: The 7.3-litre, six-cylinder engine is still purring smoothly and is capable of doing around 15 miles to the gallon.

Unique: This 100-year-old Silver Ghost Rolls Royce has sold for a world-record price of 5 million Pounds after a furious bidding war at Bonhams.

**

Quotation from Hitler

"The doom of a nation can be averted only by a storm of flowing passion, but only those who are passionate themselves can arouse passion in others."

I'm old and I'm Tired

By Robert A. Hall

Except for one semester in college when jobs were scarce and a six-month period when I was between jobs, but job-hunting every day, I've worked hard since I was 18. Despite some health challenges, I still put in 50-hour weeks, and haven't called in sick in seven or eight years. I make a good salary, but I didn't inherit my job or my income, and I worked to get where I am. Given the economy, there's no retirement in sight, and I'm tired. Very tired.

I'm tired of being told that I have to "spread the wealth" to people who don't have my work ethic. I'm tired of being told the government will take the money I'earned, by force if necessary, and give it to other people.

I'm tired of being told I must lower my living standard to fight global warming, which no one is allowed to debate.

I'm tired of being told that drug addicts have a disease, and I must help support and treat them, and pay for the damage they do. Did a giant germ rush out of a dark alley, grab them, and stuff white powder up their noses while they tried to fight it off?

I'm tired of hearing wealthy athletes, entertainers and politicians of both parties talking about innocent mistakes, stupid mistakes or youthful mistakes, when we all know they think their only mistake was getting caught. I'm tired of people with a sense of entitlement, rich or poor.

Story Telling Seventeen

I'm real tired of people who don't take responsibility for their lives and actions. I'm tired of hearing them blame the government, or discrimination or big … whatever, for their problems.

Yes, I'm damn tired. But I'm also glad to be 83, because, mostly, I'm not going to have to see the world these people are making. I'm just sorry for my granddaughters and grandson.

Robert A. Hall is a Marine Vietnam Veteran who served five terms in the Massachusetts State Senate.

**

A New SIM

Woman buys a new Sim Card. Puts it in her phone and decides to surprise her husband who is seated on the couch in the living room. She goes to the kitchen, calls her husband with the new number:

"Hello Darling."

The husband responds in a low tone:

"Let me call you back later Honey, my wife is in the kitchen.

Portrait

Richard Seal

1928

The sisters' childhood power play, operating through the veneer of democracy, was reflected in Neapolitan ice cream shared. The younger sister, Gill, whinge whined for strawberry scoops, jumping through hoops, with terror tantrums on the verge of being thrown. When she blew up, the objections were renewed as her screams turned shriller at seeing too much vanilla. Her elder sister, Sally, accepted extra chocolate without any objection, playing a long game: she had known her time would come soon for so much better confections.

1933

So bright and sharp, Sally teetered on the edge of her teens: one moment she could be sulky, another witty, then wracked with insecurity and doubt, toughed out, her laugh stuttered, eyes shuttered. She frowned down at her kid sister, irritated by her noise, confused, somewhat bemused by their bond. Gill would whirl, limbs flailing in a dance frenzy with her imaginary friend. She spoke to herself with passion and verve. The colour of this little girl was just starting to show through.

1938

Sally had been so pleased to get a job in the Civil Service working as a personal secretary. She loved reading the classics in her free time and also wrote some short stories and poetry. However, she needed to be careful to keep her work hidden from her sister, especially since their big row. Gill had responded angrily to Sally's silent treatment by scoffing her Easter Eggs one after another until vomiting molten brown buttons ... but what right did the silly girl have to read her big sister's diary and laugh about it with her friends? Gill was so childish, when she had been told that her boyfriend had been spotted kissing her best friend, she had attacked mother's box of birthday chocolates - coffee creams and hazelnut clusters were chomped amid hot streams of tears!

1947 until 1986
As adults, the sisters met in a town centre cafe once a month. The place changed hands several times over the years, and seemed to lose more of its charm on each occasion. Gill had never been too keen on the place, but Sally had always argued that the cream cakes were so good and not too dear. Every time they sat together the look on each woman's face revealed that each of them knew their place: The first-born was serene, unruffled at the scene: She arrived at dead on three and sat silently stirring her tea. The younger, running late, was always in a flustered state and seemed to be battling some minor illness or other; she would have coffee with a snack, but she needed to get back.

Story Telling Seventeen

1998

The sisters sat smiling in plaits and check skirts in the oversized picture, which had hung in pride of place in their parents' hall - the girls remained eleven and seven for years. As a teenager, the eldest had placed all the blame on Squirt for their cringing shame - she had made the picture even worse with her dirty knees and that flowery purse. Still living in the same house seven decades on, Sally stares into the sepia, travelling back to that scene often so that her dear sister, long deceased, can be beside her again.

**

Digs

The use of 'digs' to describe lodging, usually of a temporary nature, first became current in the USA where the word started out in the longer form of 'diggings' the temporary accommodation of gold miners during the Californian gold rush. The word began to be used in the U.K: in the nineteenth century.

**

A Telephone Affair

The new Minister to the Parish asked the elders who were gathered around him if there were any persons in the district who were particularly in need of his prayers. One of those present, an elderly well-dressed man said "there is old Mrs. Brown in constant pain from her arthritis, also the widow Mackintosh with her eight little ones" ... he paused before continuing "regrettable I should mention Mary ... she is a young woman with elastic virtue who's favours are bestowed ... I am sorry I have said enough." He shrugged his shoulders as his voice drained away.

The following week the New Minister was on his way to the library when he met the young woman who he easily recognised by the description he had been given, drawing a deep breath he said. "My dear I am your new Minister and I have heard all about you. I just want you to know in the few days I have been here I have been praying regularly for you."

Mary looked at him with surprise and with a smile on her face replied "Oh Minister that is kind of you, but you should not have bothered I'm on the telephone..."

**

You'll like this one! It's made from an anti-diuretic hybrid grape and reduces the number of trips people your age go to the toilet during the night.
It's called PINO MORE!

Trying On

Richard Seal

Struggling under the weight of several bags, Mark shifted his weight from one of his flat feet to the other and endeavoured to lean back against a rack of jackets without causing it to collapse. The gents' toilets were out of order and he was not sure if he could get away with popping into the ladies' without being noticed. He would rather have been almost anywhere else on a hot Saturday afternoon at the end of August than in a busy clothes shop.

He reflected that he had hated shopping since childhood, especially when it involved trying any clothes on. To this day, he still loathes the sensation of trousers pinching flesh, trying to squeezing over his thighs, and feeling so ashamed and blaming himself for being super-sized. He felt a little puzzled, but smiled seeing his daughter's joy as she headed for the changing rooms without any signs of gloom. Rosie did not look depressed at the prospect of sampling skirts or a summer dress.

Moving on to the shoe shop, Mark shuddered at memories of the end of the summer holidays and dreaded trips with his mum to buy sensible shoes for school. He felt and still feels such a fool in these places. The grim assistants armed with shoe horns had seemed resolved to raise his embarrassment levels. What made

Story Telling Seventeen

matters worse was that he had been cursed when suffering blushing seeing a girl from his class just as his mother decided to tell him off ...

Mark decides to take pity on his daughter. He grabs the first pair of acceptable-looking shoes in her size to hand, hoping his wife will understand. Suddenly noticing that Rosie looks a little disappointed to be leaving the shop so quickly, he now begins to wonder whether she shares his deeply-held view that returning to school next day is so unfair ... Surely she will appreciate skipping the scheduled visit to the hairdresser for an impromptu visit to the fair?

**

For Luxury Travel.

GIDEA PARK COACHES

LTD.

ROMFORD 2777-2778
LAINDON   67
THORNEBOURNE 2336

Tours and Excursions to all Seaside Resorts, Race Meetings, Whipsnade & Aldershot Tattoo.

Romford Coach Station, London Rd., ROMFORD

Reproduced for the Romford

PRIVATE PARTIES CATERED FOR.

Wind

Living in the country, beauty,
peace, tranquility is unreal,
almost surreal for city folk ..
But nature, noticing a cozy
complacency creeping in
around vistas, then steps in
with wild winds whipped up
as if lost at sea, fit to shift,
lift fences, collapse a shed.
Likes to hurl tiles, cut power
to keep us all in our place ..
See if we still love the stars
with a tree lying on our car.

Richard Seal

Beautiful Game

Feels so amused watching 'The Beautiful Game'
reminding him still of a sole claim to fame.
At school he was always the last to be picked
for any sports team - he felt anxious and sick.

He finished in last place in each running race,
limped over the line so entirely shamefaced.
In a twelve man team he was always thirteen.
The teasing relentless, vindictive and mean.

Then one football team, so incredibly short
threw him into midfield to disgusted retorts.
Both sides were shocked seeing drama unfold:
He went on to score the game's solitary goal!

Richard Seal

The Proposal

A young woman brought her fiancé home to meet her parents. After dinner, her mother told the girl's father to find out all about the young man. The father invited the fiancé to his study for a talk. "So, what are your plans?" the father asked the young man.

"I am a biblical scholar," he replied

"A biblical scholar, hmmm?" the father said. "Admirable; but what will you do to provide a nice house for my daughter to live in?" "I will study," the young man replied, "and God will provide for us."

"And how will you buy her a beautiful engagement ring, such as she deserves?" asked the father. "I will concentrate on my studies," the young man replied, "God will provide for us."

"And children?" asked the father. "How will you support children?" "Don't worry, sir. God will provide," replied the fiancé.

The conversation proceeded like this and each time the father raised a question, the young idealist insisted that God would provide.

Later, the mother asked, "How did your talk go, honey?" The father answered, "Just another Greens voter. He has no job, he has no plans and he thinks I'm God."

Last Man
Richard Seal

The funeral notice stopped Fred dead in his tracks -
So, Bill had succumbed to his third heart attack ...
The Big C had claimed John back in ninety one
Mike suffered a stroke - next day he was gone

He cast his mind back a half century and more
to The Cradley Heath Kids - the incredible four
So fearless all, rambling and scrambling at will
through woods, heavy undergrowth, steepest of hills

So often regarded as the weakest of links,
the last man left standing now needed a drink
This snivelling lad often left holding coats
had become adept writing obituary notes.

Clouds
Richard Seal
Looking up from plate, the fork
suspended a moment, he gazes
out of his window at the clouds;
purses lips and frowns in breeze ..
Adjectives are not up to scratch -
fluffy, puffy, and cotton will not do.
Clouds look like potato, mashed,
gravy-streaked, threatening rain;
while hailstones are these peas ...

In Days of Old (as seen Now!)

Nelson: "Order the signal, Hardy."

Hardy: "Aye, aye sir."

Nelson: "Hold on, this isn't what I dictated to Flags. What's the meaning of this?"

Hardy: "Sorry sir?"

Nelson (reading aloud): "England expects every person to do his or her duty, regardless of race, gender, sexual orientation, religious persuasion or disability - What gobbledygook is this for God's sake?"

Hardy: "Admiralty policy, I'm afraid, sir. We're an equal opportunities employer now. We had the devil's own job getting "England" past the censors, lest it be considered racist."

Nelson: "Gadzooks, Hardy. Hand me my pipe and tobacco."

Hardy: "Sorry Sir. All naval vessels have now been designated smoke-free working environments."

Nelson: "In that case, break open the rum ration Let us splice the main brace to steel the men before battle."

Hardy: "The rum ration has been abolished, Admiral. It's part of the Government's policy on binge drinking."

Nelson: "Damn it man! We are on the eve of the greatest sea battle in history. We must advance with all dispatch. Report from the crow's nest, please."

Hardy: "That won't be possible, sir."

Nelson: "What?"

Hardy: "Health and Safety have closed the crow's nest, sir. No harness; and they said that rope ladders don't meet regulations They won't let anyone up there until proper scaffolding can be erected"

Nelson: "Then get me the ship's carpenter without delay, Hardy."

Story Telling Seventeen

Hardy: "He's busy knocking up a wheelchair access to the foredeck Admiral."

Nelson: "Wheelchair access? I've never heard anything so absurd."

Hardy: "Health and safety again, sir. We have to provide a barrier-free environment for the differently abled."

Nelson: "Differently abled? I've only one arm and one eye and I refuse even to hear mention of the word. I didn't rise to the rank of admiral by playing the disability card."

Hardy: "Actually, sir, you did. The Royal Navy is under-represented in the areas of visual impairment and limb deficiency."

Nelson: "I've never heard such infamy. Break out the cannon and tell the men to stand by to engage the enemy."

Hardy: "The men are a bit worried about shooting at anyone, Admiral."

Nelson: "What? This is mutiny!"

Hardy: "It's not that, sir. It's just that they're afraid of being charged with murder if they actually kill anyone. There are a couple of legal-aid lawyers on board, watching everyone like hawks."

Nelson: "Then how are we to sink the French and the Spanish?"

Hardy: "Actually, sir, we're not."

Nelson: "We're not?"

Hardy: "No, Sir. The French and the Spanish are our European partners now. According to the Common Fisheries Policy, we shouldn't even be in this stretch of water. We could get hit with a claim for compensation."

Nelson: "But you must hate a Frenchman as you hate the devil."

Hardy: "I wouldn't let the ship's diversity coordinator hear you saying that Sir. You'll be up on disciplinary report."

Story Telling Seventeen

Nelson: "You must consider every man an enemy, who speaks ill of your King."

Hardy: "Not any more, sir. We must be inclusive in this multicultural age. Now put on your Kevlar vest; it's the rules. It could save your life"

Nelson: "Don't tell me - Health and Safety. Whatever happened to rum, sodomy and the lash?"

Hardy: "As I explained, sir, rum is off the menu! And there's a ban on corporal punishment."

Nelson: "What about homosexuality?"

Hardy: "I believe that is now legal, sir, let's hope it doesn't become compulsory "

Nelson: "In that case.............. Kiss me, Hardy."

Did you know that having sex while drunk is banned in Iceland .. not sure about asda you will have to check their rules

The following is the opening Chapter to
'Death for a Starter'
by Percy W. Chattey

The novel is the first part of a trilogy and is followed by 'The Dauntless Factor' and 'The Cormack's'

Chapter One
The Mid Eighteen Hundreds

Mid eighteen hundreds Ireland
The O'Dowd's Small Holding

Alicia was desperate as she searched for food for her two children, Patrick and Florence. The ground was wet and very muddy. Her feet were icy, in shoes which were badly worn, giving little protection against the bitter cold. She was digging with her bare hands and holding a medium size sharp pointed knife to help in moving the soil to one side, trying to find a potato that had survived the blight. With a heavy heart she could see the fungus had spread across the plot of land, and that the leaves had wilted turning to a dirty looking brown with round blackish spots. Although knowing it was useless, with her husband and son, both of whom were on other areas of the patch of ground, continuing their search for just one of the vegetables which had survived the disease.

She was feeling very tired, as it was almost a week since Alicia had eaten a fulfilling meal and the lack of proper food was starting to tell on her health. She looked up and her heart missed a beat as Reuben was holding up something, and in that moment Alicia knew he had found one that had survived the infection.

It had started to rain in a soft drizzle, like a heavy mist, as he started to make his way towards her. Tears flooded her eyes as she looked at the man she loved, and saw what the years, this terrible food shortage and constant worry had done to him. When they had married ten years previously they had so much hope. She had expected to continue the life she had had with her parents, living in luxury without having to work. In those days he was a strong man who stood tall – right now as he staggered across the field he was stooped, dressed in rags with mud over his legs and arms, looking far older than his years.

The hope vanished from her when she saw what he had in his hand. Although a full size potato she knew in her heart as soon as they cut into it the flesh would be inedible. Large tears ran down her cheeks as she flung her arms around him and cried on his shoulder. The rain adding to their depression as the cold water fell on each head and ran down the back of their necks.

Story Telling Seventeen

"Mather" - it was their son Patrick. He like them had been working on another part of the small holding and he was calling beside the little cottage they called home. The stone built structure with its thatched roof was not very secure against the weather, a small building like so many others that had been built across the Irish countryside. Inside were just two tiny rooms where they lived, straw mattresses on the floor at night and during the day rickety wooden furniture littered the rooms for comfort of the barest minimum. In one corner was a small fireplace, which was rarely lit, as they could not afford to buy the fuel for it, and what kindling they could find in the fields surrounding them, was too wet to light for the warmth of a fire.

From the far side of their home she could see a well-dressed man on a black horse which was travelling down the narrow path. She knew at once it was the Land Agent, the man responsible for collecting rent and to do the bidding of the English Landlord. But this was a person she did not recognise. She turned and looked at her husband, "Who is he? What do you think he wants?"

"It has to be somebody about the rent and no doubt to check on the growth of their hay." Because they could not afford to pay rent the Landlord had allowed them to supply him with produce, which they had to grow from their own resources.

"But the growth has been so poor because of the foul weather - also I can't help feeling that the potato blight has something to do with it. What can we do?" Alicia was frightened and knew this was not going to be good news.

A rare smile crossed his lips, "We have got nothing more to offer them." He took hold of her hand as they turned to struggle in the mud to the cottage.

Story Telling Seventeen

The agent was a burly man who was smartly dressed in shiny boots and a leather jacket. He was holding a sword at his side as he dismounted from the horse, a completely black mare.

Once on the ground, he looked at them in distaste and turning, he took a board out of the pannier strapped to the horse behind the saddle. He looked at the paper attached to the board. "You have some land where your kind landlord has allowed you to grow hay instead of paying him rent. I need to see it, where is it?"

Reuben was shaking his head, "The seeds need some warmth for it to grow, it will look better when the weather changes." He had started to walk to one side of the cottage.

The agent was not pleased with what he saw, "Is this all?"

"Yes. When our farm was taken from us and we were told to farm this...(he waved his hands at the plot)...but the ground is too poor to grow crops on..." He wanted to shout at the man but knew it would be useless and would not help, instead his voice sounded weary and without conviction.

The agent turned and slapped him across the face. "How dare you, you ungrateful people. That grass had better recover very soon and be ready for the scythe." He then walked quickly to another part of their ground.

Alicia could feel the temper building inside her as she followed, the knife still in her right hand tucked out of sight up the rags of a sleeve.

"As you are not producing enough to pay the rent, this area will need to be turned into hay." He was pointing to a small plot on which a small skinny cow was grazing, the animal supplied the family with enough milk for them so they could survive.

Story Telling Seventeen

"But that is not possible. Where would the animal go? There is no other place." Alicia was nodding her head as she listened to her husband.

"That is not our problem. You entered into an agreement, now stick to it." He turned to walk back to the horse, tucking the board under his arm, pushing Reuben out of the way as he did so. Reuben muttered "Forced into an agreement more like!"

Alicia moved and stood in front of him, "I suppose it does not matter to you if we die of starvation, as my Mother and Father did last year. All you want is our food and to leave us with nothing." She was talking slowly with tears running down her cheeks. She could not remember being so angry and furious at what this man was saying. She also knew, like so many others they would not be able to continue to exist, which they were barely doing now. Without the feeble milk they were getting from the cow they would have nothing, and her children would suffer. It flashed through her mind - in that case why should he not suffer as well?

She stood her ground as he moved forward. She could hear her husband telling her to move out of his way. She shouted at the agent, "How do I feed the bairns? Eh! Go on tell me."

He was looking down at her grinning, "That is nothing to do with me," before he could say anything more she swung her right hand upwards. The knife, which she had been holding in her fist, with the blade held along her wrist could not be seen under the pieces of cloth she was wearing. Suddenly she reversed it, the blade flashed as she forced it upwards. There was a hesitation as it tried to penetrate the leather of the jacket. Using more vigour, the knife continued, the sharp pointed end went easily into him and continued up under his ribs.

There was no noise, just blood gushing out over the blade and her hand. With a surprised look on his face the agent silently dropped to the ground. Reuben looked at her astounded wondering what had happened; she was still standing and looking down in shock. She watched as Patrick pulled the blade from the visitor's chest, blood covering his hand and more on the rags he was wearing.

The agent lying on the ground had not moved. The couple standing beside the body were looking at each other, both wondering how it had happened whilst knowing they were in deep trouble.

There was a scream - Florence, their daughter had come out of the shack and was standing near them shivering, and starting to cry. Her mother took her in her arms rocking her and whilst still looking at her husband, her mind was in a whirl, knowing if and when the authorities found out they would all be hanged for murder.

Alicia in her heart knew what she had done was wicked, but what the man had intended was equally so, condemning a family to die from starvation like many others in that terrible time for Ireland. They both knew that now they had a death on their hands they would have to make a new start.

**

Quotation from Hitler
"Never trust a person who isn't having at least one crisis."

Droning On.

This was Percy's blog published in December 2018 after Gatwick Airport was closed at the height of the travelling season following the interruption by Drones over the runways...

We are told the Home Secretary has had a bad couple of weeks, which did not stop him from going on safari for the Christmas Break, although he has now hurried back to try and sort out the problem of the invasion of small boats crossing the English Channel by immigrants.

In the mean time we learn that the spectacle of the events at Gatwick Airport a few days ago was a mistake when ninety two trusted informers of the police reported drones over the runways, which in all possibilities will turn out to be warning lights on high builder's cranes swaying in the wind, as seen from seven miles away.

In a situation which Rowan Atkinson would have been proud to have written in one of his humorous sketches, the Police send up a drone to look for the supposed illegal ones. Now there are real flying objects crisscrossing the airport and no one got to grips with the situation and realised the ones that were now flying were friendly ones and not there to disrupt the flight time tables.

The Police having refused help from the Armed Forces chase around looking for persons launching these flying objects and resort to knowledge of known people who like the pastime of flying toy aeroplanes and manage to arrest a couple who had nothing to do with it. On further investigation, so we are told, no evidence could be found of drones being launched from anywhere around the airport.

While this is happening hundreds of thousands of passengers look at departure boards and the disappointing word 'cancelled' for 750 flights and fretting if they will get to their Christmas destination, and out of frustration and lack of sleep, curl up on the cold floor, while they wait for the problem to be sorted.

While writing a fictional story, if I had thought of something similar, it is a situation I would have discarded as being unbelievable. Story telling has to have a level of excitement and drama, but to close a main terminus down for 36 hours does not seem possible in a fictional tale not in the circumstances as portrayed, and my guess is the reader would put the book down at that point. It goes to show life is stranger than fiction.

H.G. Wells

By Richard Seal

"We all have our time machines, don't we? Those that take us back are memories...And those that carry us forward, are dreams." - H.G. Wells

Visionary writer H.G. Wells was born Herbert George Wells on September 21, 1866, in Bromley, England. After his father's shop failed, the family struggled financially. His mother went to work on an estate as a housekeeper. Wells discovered the owner's extensive library. He read the works of Jonathan Swift and some of the important figures of the Enlightenment.

In his early teens, Wells went to work as a draper's assistant, like his brothers.

He won a scholarship to the Normal School of Science and also devoted much of his time to becoming a writer. Whilst at college, he published a short story about time travel called "The Chronic Argonauts." After graduating he turned his attention to teaching. In 1895, Wells became an overnight literary sensation with the publication of his novel "The Time Machine". The book explored social and scientific topics, from class conflict to evolution, themes which were to recur in some of his other works.

Story Telling Seventeen

In quick succession, he published "The Island of Doctor Moreau" (1896), "The Invisible Man" (1897) and "The War of the Worlds" (1898). On Halloween night 1938, Orson Welles went on the air with his version of the latter, claiming that aliens had landed in New Jersey. In addition to fiction, Wells wrote many essays, articles and nonfiction. In 1901, he published "Anticipations", in which he forecasted the rise of major cities, economic globalization, and aspects of future military conflicts.

For a time, the writer was a member of the Fabien Society, and he explored issues of social class and economic disparity in a number of his works, including "Kipps" (1905). He wrote a number of other comic novels of lower middle-class life, most notably "The History of Mr. Polly" (1910). In these works Wells revealed the hopes and frustrations of clerks, shop assistants, and teachers, with sympathetic understanding.

In 1920, Wells published "The Outline of History". This three-volume work began with prehistory and followed world events up through The Great War. Around this time, he also tried to advance his political ideas, unsuccessfully running for Parliament as a Labour Party candidate in 1922 and 1923. He branched out into film in the 1930s, adapting his 1933 novel "The Shape of Things to Come" for the screen, and also worked on the film version of his short story, "The Man Who Could Work Miracles."

The writer travelled widely. He visited Russia in 1920 where he met Vladimir Lenin and Leon Trotsky. The following decade he had the opportunity to talk with Josef Stalin and American president Franklin D. Roosevelt. He lectured and went on speaking tours, gaining notoriety for his radical social and political views. Taking a break from wartime London in 1940, Wells came to the United States, where he delivered a talk entitled "Two Hemispheres—One World."

For five decades, H.G. devoted his life to writing and he was very prolific. Among his last works was 1945's "Mind at the End of Its Tether," a pessimistic essay in which he contemplates the end of humanity. At the time of his death, in August 1946, Wells was remembered as a author, historian and champion of certain social and political ideals. Today the man is best known as "the Father of Science Fiction" and his stories continue to fascinate contemporary audiences.

Wells was able to reflect the energy of the period, and its feeling of release from the conventions of Victorian times. In his efforts for social equality, world peace, and what he considered to be the future good of humanity, he had a huge influence on his own generation and on those to follow. Several of his works have returned to the cinema in recent years, including the 2005 remake of "War of the Worlds", featuring Tom Cruise and Dakota Fanning as two of the people fighting to survive the alien invasion.

"Sometimes, you have to step outside of the person you've been and remember the person you were meant to be. The person you want to be. The person you are."

H.G. Wells

**

A MAN went to the movies and was surprised to find a woman with a big collie sitting in front of him. Even more amazing was the fact that the dog always laughed in the right places through the comedy.

"Excuse me," the man said to the

woman, "but I think it's astounding that your dog enjoys the movie so much."

"I'm surprised myself," she replied. "He hated the book."

Story Telling Seventeen

On hearing the anguished cries of children from the street, one of Abraham Lincoln's neighbours rushed out of his house in alarm. He found his fellow citizen with his two sons both of whom were sobbing uncontrollably. "Whatever is the matter with the boys Mr. Lincoln? He asked. "Just what is the matter with the whole world," was the reply resignedly, "I've got three walnuts, and each wants two of them."

**

Behind every stack of books is a flood of knowledge.
-Eddie Conlon

Hoarder

Richard Seal

Jenny moved the pile of magazines on the settee over a little to accommodate her ashtray. She stood up slowly and shuffled through the living room, edging slowly around the stacked cardboard boxes and stepping over the plates and cups on the floor. Before the woman had the chance to squeeze her way through the door, she heard the doorbell ring. For a moment she toyed with the idea of ignoring it, but a familiar voice put paid to that.

"Hello Mum it's Maggie, let me in!"

Jenny trudged to the door, and opened it to find her middle aged daughter looking as harassed as ever.

"Hello, dear."

Maggie kissed her mother briefly, but quickly turned her attention to the state of the house. "I know I haven't been here for a while, but this place looks worse than ever! There is rubbish everywhere, no room to move. How can you stand it? What do you need these things for?" She picked up one of several carrier bags lined up in the hall.

"This is my house, and these are my things. Please put the bag down." Jenny's voice quavered, and her hand shook slightly as she reached out to Maggie.

"Fine, I might catch something!" She dropped the bag. She took a deep breath and tried to calm herself down. "Look Mum, this isn't normal. I don't think you're well."

"Stop patronising me, I know what I'm doing. If you want to call me a hoarder, go ahead. I'm not doing anyone any harm."

"Yes, but .."

"Have you come to see me or to give a lecture? I don't tell you how to live your life, do I?"

The two women settled on a tense truce and managed to find a little space to have a cup of tea at the kitchen table. The conversation was perfunctory, until Maggie got up to leave. Frowning hard, she put her hand on the old woman's arm.

"I'm sorry that I got angry, Mum, it's just that I care and worry about you. Especially since Dad died."

The lady nodded and patted her hand gently "I know you do, love, but I'm fine. I appreciate that the house isn't very tidy, but I am quite happy here."

After her daughter had gone, Jenny left the used cups on the table, and draped a tea cloth over them. She lit a cigarette as her mind settled on Derek. Thoughts had never strayed too far from her husband in the five years since he had passed away. A smile spread across her face, accompanied by a few tears as she negotiated her way back into the living room to search for a TV programme that they had enjoyed together. Only half the screen was visible due to the heap of newspapers nearby.

Story Telling Seventeen

Jenny had been on the waiting list for an operation for several months. When the date was finally confirmed, Maggie tried to put the anxious lady's mind at rest by reassuring her that the house would be fine without her for a few days. She stressed she would leave things as they were, and just check the post a couple of times. However, she had decided to spring a nice surprise on her mother - With the help of two friends, she cleaned the place from top to bottom and filled two skips with the obvious junk, putting the other things into some kind of order and away into cupboards and drawers wherever possible.

Maggie had not expected such an underwhelming response to all her efforts. Her mother seemed to be struck dumb by the shock of arriving back to a neat and tidy house. After standing in complete silence for several minutes, Jenny had managed to mumble a few words of thanks, but said very little else as she slumped down onto the settee and stared into space. It was only after her daughter had made her excuses and left, that the old woman finally allowed herself to break down and cry uncontrollably.

Over the next few weeks, Maggie noticed that her mother was either not returning her calls or making excuses as to why it was not convenient for her to come round. However, eventually Jenny told her daughter that she wanted to get out of the house a bit more and suggested they meet at a cafe for coffee and a chat once a week. It turned out to be a great idea, as the two women seemed to get along better than they had done for years. The old lady was feeling so much more secure and at ease now that her precious things were all around her again, back in view in their rightful places.

**

Snow

It was snowing heavily and blowing to the point where visibility was down to zero by the time Debbie left work one evening. She just made it to her car but was worried how she was going to get home.

She sat in her car while it warmed and considered her situation and finally recalled some advise her father had given her, if she was ever in a blizzard and stuck in deep snow wait for a snow plough to come along and follow it, by doing this it would reduce her chances of being stuck in a snow drift.

This made her feel better, she waited in the warm car and eventually a snow plough went past. Debbie feeling very smug as she had solved her problem with the blizzard and the snow followed it.

After travelling some considerable distance behind the snow plough she was surprised when it stopped. The driver got out and came over to her car indicating for her to lower the window. He asked her if she was alright as she had been following him for some time. She said she was fine and told him of her father's advise that if caught in a blizzard to follow a snow plough.

The driver said that was good advice and it was Okay with him and she could continue to follow him if she wanted to. She said she was grateful and would follow him as he didn't mind. He nodded his head and told her that now he had finished the Asda car park he was moving on to the Tesco one.

**

"Honesty must be the best policy, but it's important to remember that apparently, by elimination, dishonesty is the second best policy."

George Carlin - Comedian and Author.

Percy's Blog and a caution about Bank Statements!

The Carbon Paper Scam.

Let me tell a little story about fraud which at one time was quite rife way back in the days when secretaries and clerks used that clattering machine, the typewriter. It would be mostly women who would spend all of the working day punching out letters, but first they had to feed a sheet of paper into the carriage and normally two sheets of carbon paper to produce copies of the work.

Let's talk about the Ford Motor Company, but then it could be any large organization. It does not take too much of an imagination to think of the masses of letters and the copies this company would produce every day, it must have run into the hundreds of thousands, letters to dealers and suppliers and of course customers.

Now some bright spark thought it was a good idea to send them an invoice for carbon paper and it became known as the 'Carbon Paper Scam'. It went on for a long time until auditors finally picked it up, for you see the invoices were for small amounts so nobody ever checked them, they just paid them, not realizing there was no order given for the stock and in fact there was no stock. It was reported the organizers of the scam got away with over a million pounds.

I'll go back to bank statements and cannot help but feel that maybe some organizations are doing something similar to its customers. Let me explain. Three years ago we took out an agreement with a software company to pay them twenty three pounds per year on the due date of February. Each year since then the payments have gone through as agreed. However this year they decided to take a second payment in May. If we did not check our bank statement every day, we would not have known about it and they would be that much richer and us that much poorer.

This is not the first time this has happened, on another occasion it was over one hundred pounds that had been wrongly debited. The point really is, was it deliberate or just a computer hitch – either way it pays to check. Why daily you may ask, well if there is a debit that should not be there then you can stop it there and then, if you leave it to the next day it is too late the bank will have paid it. On one occasion we found a thousand pounds was missing but I think we would have noticed that anyway. **I wonder how many people are having money debited as a regular payment,** *which they know nothing about? Take care!*
www.percychatteybooks.com

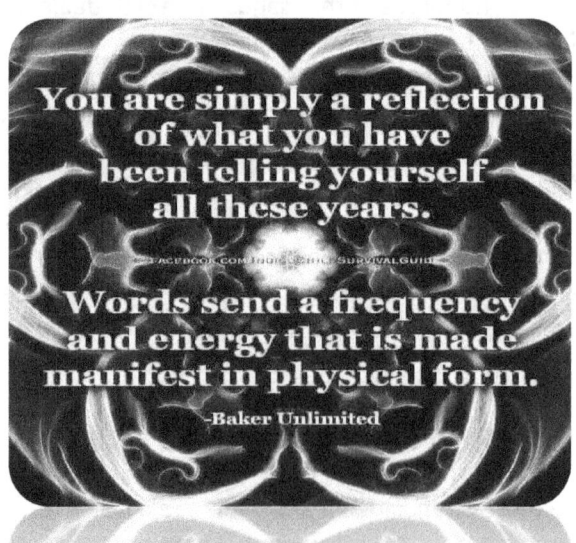

A Plan Is Put In Place
Terry Tumbler
Chapter Two
From the Novel *Santiago Tales*
by Terry Tumbler. Chapter One and the start of the journey was published in Story Telling Sixteen.

Terry and John were pleasantly surprised by the number of applications they had received to join them in their pilgrimage to Santiago de Compostela.

"Right, let's choose an intended start date and itinerary for this pilgrimage," Terry said briskly. "I fancy the end of June or thereabouts, lasting for a duration of sixteen days. Now, I have in my hands a copy of the splendid itinerary submitted by my preferred tour operator, *Santiago Pathways*. Read this extract:"

What is included:

Pre-departure information

Experienced guides to accompany the group

Support vehicle

All ground transportation to and from fixed points of departure, and from the start of the pilgrimage in León to the finish in Santiago de Compostela.

The Pilgrim's Passport, daily maps and descriptions of the sections to be walked.

Day 1 – Origin /León

> *Arrive in León. We'll begin with a visit to some of the*
> *most emblematic points in the city, such as the*
> *cathedral and the Basílica de San Isidoro, an elegantly*
> *compact and solid example of the Spanish*
> *Romanesque.*

Story Telling Seventeen

Day 2 – León - Villadangos del Páramo (21.8 kms)

As with many of the other villages that we will encounter along the Camino Francés, this little village owed its former prestige to the Camino's existence. Our halt here puts us within a day's walk of the ancient Roman city of Astorga, our destination for tomorrow.

Day 3 – Villadangos del Páramo – Astorga (27.1 kms)

Asturica Augustus was an important communications hub for the Romans and the most important city of this region of Spain, known as the Maragatería. We will enjoy a relaxed dinner in the restored city centre and attend Mass in the cathedral.

Day 4 –Astorga - Rabanal del Camino (20.7 kms)

Today we journey through the plains of Castile and León and enter the mountains of León. The monks who live here discovered their vocation on the Camino de Santiago and were later granted permission by their abbot to found a new monastery on the route to attend to the spiritual needs of pilgrims. Tonight we will have a hearty supper in one of the local bars.

Day 5 – Rabanal del camino –Molinaseca (33 kms)

Our day's journey begins with a walk to the semi-abandoned village of Foncebadón and, just beyond it, to the Cruz de Ferro (Iron Cross), one of the contemporary Camino's most emblematic points and the highest point on the Camino (1,500 metres, or 4,921 (feet). Afterwards, our descent of the mountain takes us to Molinaseca, a lovely riverside village.

Story Telling Seventeen

Day 6 – Molinaseca - Cacabelos (23.5 kms)
This morning we enter Ponferrada, capital of the El Bierzo region of Spain. Its name derives from its bridge which stretches over the River Sil. It was the home to the Templar Knights, sworn to the protection of pilgrims travelling the Way of St. James. Their imposing castle still stands, and has become the emblem of the city. Stay overnight at Cacabelos.

Day 7 – Cacabelos – Villafranca del Bierzo (7.2 kms) or Vega de Valcarce)
Today's journey will be short. Villafranca del Bierzo has always offered the pilgrims wonderful hospitality and an advantageous point from which to begin the next day's ascent to O Cebreiro.

Day 8 – Villafranca del Bierzo - O Cebreiro (30.3 kms)
Today's destination is one of the most memorable along the entire Camino. With its stunning vistas of the valleys below from 1300 metres up, the ancient pallozas (pre-Roman stone dwellings built by the Celts of the region)... few places along the Camino are as enchanting as O Cebreiro!

Day 9 – O Cebreiro - Triacastela (Samos) (20.4 kms)
The lush valleys and rolling green hills of Galicia, Spain's Celtic region, bear more than a little resemblance to Ireland. Nestled in a tranquil valley, our destination today is Triacastela, founded in the 9th century following the reconquest of this the area from the Muslims. Today nothing remains of the three castles that gave the village its name.

Story Telling Seventeen

Day 10 – Triacastela (Samos) - Sarria (21.5kms)

Our journey today ends in Sarria, the site of an ancient Roman settlement that was repopulated in the 8th century by Bishop Odoario of Lugo. It is an excellent place to rest and enjoy the wonderful seafood offered in one of the many taverns on the promenade along the banks of the river.

Day 11 – Sarria - Portomarín (21.6kms)

Just before Portomarín today we pass the 100 kilometer mark on the Camino, the minimum point from which anyone travelling to Santiago must walk in order to receive the Compostela.
The Portomarín in which we will sleep tonight is not the Portomarín that pilgrims in the Middle Ages knew; that one lies below the waters of the reservoir we see in the valley below.

Día 12 –Portomarin - Palas do Rei (24.5kms)

Palas de Rei, is a friendly and welcoming place, and it's where we'll make our halt today.
The town's name (Palace of the King) derives from a legend that says that the Visigothic king Witiza built the town's palace. Just as it was in the Middle Ages, the village is surrounded by numerous small farming villages.

Day 13 – Palas de Rei -Arzúa (28.7 kms)

Our journey today ends at the little village of Arzúa, famous for its cheeses. A cheese festival is held here every year in March. En route we'll pass through the bustling small town of Melide, once an important intersection in the Roman Via Traiana and the northern roads descending from the Cantabrian coast.

Day 14 – Arzúa - Lavacolla (28.8 kms)
Our journey today ends in Lavacolla, a tiny village only 10 kilometers (6.2 miles) from our goal, and well positioned so that we may make an early entrance into Santiago tomorrow morning.

Day 15 – Lavacolla - Santiago de Compostela (10.3kms)
We will reach Santiago de Compostela well before the 12.00 Pilgrim's Mass in the cathedral. If we are lucky, the gigantic botafumeiro censer will be used during the Mass. Afterwards we will head over to the Pilgrim's Office to receive our Compostelas.Overnight stop at a quiet hotel in the old quarter.

Day 16 – departure from Santiago de Compostela
You will have up to a couple of hours free to explore the city, relax, shop for souvenirs and pray in the cathedral. Afterwards, you will depart by coach to your original pick-up points.

"The total is 319.4 kilometres. Does that sound doable to you, my old fruit?"
John replied doubtfully, saying "Er, perhaps yes, provided everyone can keep up! Remember, many of us are in our seventies, so…"
"Ah, I have a plan!" Terry said. "We'll have a minibus hovering in the neighbourhood as we progress, ready to pick up strays who have fallen by the wayside, as well as transport the weaker of both sexes who accompany us, *and* we'll have a

proper guide walking with us to point out the attractions en route."

Terry asked him, "Could you cross-check with me who wants to come?" John looked at his list and passed across the details. So far they had,

Brett, a retired Salesman, accompanied by

Susan, his wife;

Billy, a retired Engineer, with

Bessie, his wife;

James Tuck, "a single, retired 'gentle man', at least, that's how he describes himself; I've met him already, and he seems to be a jovial, inoffensive character";

Graham, a retired soldier, with

Norma, his wife;

Jon, a retired garage workshop owner, with

Barbara, his wife;

John, a computer contractor, "who's coming on his own";

Syd, a retired Air-conditioning engineering, accompanied by

Maggie, his wife, a retired cook;

Mick, a retired lorry driver, with

Janis, his wife;

Ted, a retired publican, with

Von, his wife, also in the trade;

Wilf Right-Angle, a retired printer, accompanied by

Prissy, his wife; "whose maiden name was originally Angle, hence the double-barrelled name that he adopted. Funny man he is";

Story Telling Seventeen

Vic, a retired paramedic "he could be useful" with
Jane, his wife, who still works for the Red Cross;

"Last but not least, we have our illustrious selves, namely,"
Terry Tumbler, retired detective, with
Sandra, his long suffering wife, "and myself,"
Dr John Watson PhD, retired librarian and current
poet, tasked with recording the stories told en
route.

Terry rubbed his hands together and proclaimed, "That's fine! I've got a few more names in the melting pot, if we need them, but if you could now match the list to the submitted letters of application and send copies off to this shortlist of competing travel agents," he handed John three replies he had received from interested agents, "and we'll see what they come up with."

"That's unfair, you've hardly done anything!" John protested. "I thought that you were going to handle the arrangements personally!"

"You know what think did," snorted Terry. "It's my trip too, and I want to enjoy it without having to cluck like Mother Goose over her brood. Besides, using professionals means I get the chance of having a substantial reduction for myself, plus they can do all the donkey work."

John shook his head in resignation. "Okay, I'll get the paperwork and contact details together and contact them." He had to admit that there was a lot of sense in getting someone else to handle arrangements and ensure that money was paid on time.

"Fine," said Terry, with a satisfied smile, while John intended ensuring that he personally would benefit from any discount he negotiated. Of course, Terry had suspected this would happen, and in his own way had prompted it.

Within a week, those hoping to join the pilgrimage found themselves dealing with a third party called *Santiago Pathways*, Terry's preferred operator, who provided glossy brochures extolling the priceless (in reality, 'pricey') value of their guided walks on the, '*Caminos Francés a Santiago de Compostela*', a detailed itinerary for the sixteen day walking-holiday, (or fourteen days if you exclude the optional extra two night hotel stays that Terry had added to the start and end of the vacation), confirmation of hotel bookings and a reasonably hefty bill for an all-in deal.

The reaction of some of the lucky recipients was a sharp intake of breath, followed by a distinctly unchristian oath and exclamation along the lines, "Well, it's that or the bloody cruise she wanted to go on!" Being cooped up on a plague ship with three thousand other inmates was not everyone's idea of Heaven.

Graham the old soldier, had wanted to leave his dearly beloved at home, rather than pay the cost of dragging her along to keep tabs on him. He'd just gained membership of Mensa, the institute for the intellectually gifted, and was buggered if he was going to meet her costs as well, having only recently found out that he could add up.

However, his wife Norma was having none of this nonsense. She knew how to handle the situation, and made him cook his own meals until he treated her with more consideration. One week and he capitulated.

Meanwhile, Terry was feeling resentful at John's assurance that his requested discount had been shared between everyone, since none of the selected travel agents could negotiate on the basis of him, Terry, being allocated a free room in high season.

Much to John's astonishment, the bookings were confirmed by all on the original list, and a coach would be collecting them from pick-up points nearest to their homes, for the trip 'oop north' in June.

When he commented on this, Terry remarked, "Actually, I'm not surprised at all by the high take-up. It's not unusual to pay a lot for a hiking holiday, and for the majority of these people it's probably their last chance in life to undertake such a venture. There are many Christians for whom the end justifies the means in this instance." John nodded in agreement, pleasantly surprised at Terry's insight; normally he was as thick-skinned as they come.

"Why are you and your pals going too, seeing as you're hardly *Christians*?" he asked, taking advantage of the opportunity to get to know Terry better.

"I've always been fascinated by these believers," he replied gruffly. "I find such people strangely nice and forgiving to be with (he meant, towards himself). Also, the scenery up there is reportedly fantastic, and me and a few mates have agreed that we want to do this journey at least once before we die:" John wondered just how lacking in certain human qualities and belief this man Tumbler really was.

And so the pilgrimage would begin.

**

Lexophillias

No matter how much you push the envelope, it'll still be stationery.

"Let us not seek the Republican answer or the Democratic answer, but the right answer. Let us not seek to fix the blame for the past. Let us accept our own responsibility for the future."

— John F. Kennedy

Witchfinder

Trudie Oakley

Josiah Adams picked his way along the narrow dirt path that snaked through a lush meadow in the Norfolk countryside. The morning dew was evaporating giving off a sweet smell from fresh new grass and spring flowers but the sombre procession that followed in his trail did not notice nature's new mantle; their mission was of a sinister nature and did not sit well with the joys of Spring. He was accompanied by John Evans who had assisted him in his efforts as Witchfinder for some years now. Straggling behind him were several villagers, the most voluble of whom was Biddy Shaw. She was the village scold, a small sharp nosed woman whose vindictive nature was evident in every line of her permanently scowling face. She had convinced the village and eventually Josiah himself that the woman they were about to call upon was a witch. Her hatred of this woman was driven by an almost insane jealousy of her beauty and popularity – she was everything that Biddy was not or could ever be. Her dislike had festered over the years until the level of hatred she felt was beyond all reason.

Josiah thought Biddy to be an obnoxious spiteful woman, but his feelings toward her were of no consequence; he was in the business of searching out witches and ridding the world of evil, and thus was obliged to investigate each and every accusation. He had more or less stumbled into his present position, and although a little unsure of himself, or indeed the validity of such an occupation, had soon realised that he could earn a decent living from it, but more than that he had become addicted to the power of life or death that he alone held over the poor wretched creatures he pursued.

Jenna watched the small party approaching. She recognised Biddy and a few others but those two gentlemen walking in front were strangers. Their black clothing and stern faces struck a chord of fear in her and her instincts told her that no good would come of this. She had come to hate Biddy Shaw – she had lived on her own since the death of her father four years ago eking out a living by growing most of her own food and taking in the odd bit of sewing but gradually friends stopped calling on her and she'd become aware of people avoiding her when she called into the village. She had been perplexed and upset at first but then she learned that Biddy Shaw had been telling tales about her and warning all the women to watch their man when such a loose woman as Jenna was about. So for the last few months she had lived the sad miserable life of a hermit with only her cat and her cow for company.

Jenna's cottage sat in the middle of a small copse and as they approached Josiah could see a shapely figure standing in the doorway; this was not what he had expected. Standing in her yard he saw that the woman was little more than a girl, and a beautiful one at that. He felt suddenly uncomfortable and the authoritative air that he usually adopted when dealing with the accused deserted him. Jenna spoke, "What can I do for you Sir?" She cast an eye over the villagers who now assiduously avoided eye contact. "If you and these good folk have business with me pray tell me what it is." She stooped to pick up her cat who was rubbing against her trembling legs.

In the absence of anything issuing from Josiah's lips Biddy Shaw chimed in "This here is the Witchfinder and he's come to put an end to you and all your evil doings. I've told him you helped deliver Martha's baby last Spring and they both died, and I've told him Robert's cow died just one day after you bathed it's wound, and there's my hens who stopped laying the day you walked across my land and I've heard you talking to that cat of yours, and...." She moved to stand directly in front of Josiah so that she could look him directly in the eye, "She was spawned by the devil she was, and make no mistake about it." Jenna watched Biddy's lips move in her twisted hateful face and was shocked at the way she spat out her words with such venom.

"But Martha died of milk fever and the baby was born sickly – you know this Biddy – why are you saying all these things?"

Josiah found his voice at last and tried to sound businesslike. The girl was delightful and he felt in his heart that she was no witch. No, this was just one spiteful old hag who probably coveted the very fine cow that stood in a small paddock, or maybe she coveted the girl's cottage – he would have to move carefully – couldn't tarnish his reputation. "You are Miss Jenna Evans, is that correct?" Jenna nodded. "I have been appointed as Witchfinder in this county of Norfolk and you have been accused of malefaction and witchcraft, and it is only right and proper that my colleague and I interrogate you and have you examined for anything that might indicate your guilt or otherwise."

Biddy smirked "I'll examine her, I know I'll find proof, I'll…."

"Thank you Mrs Shaw but I think 'tis best to have someone from the village other than the accuser – all examinations must be thorough and above board and I need to maintain my reputation of fairness and accuracy." He turned to Jenna, "You will need to come with us right now, I have already spoken to the vicar's wife who has agreed to assist us in our endeavours and she is awaiting our return."

Jenna knew it was futile to argue – it may go against her. She picked up her cat and kissed her on the head whispering in her ear, "Pray for me Sophia, pray for me." The small party retraced their steps in single file with Jenna walking in front of Josiah and he was intoxicated by the nearness of her. He watched the sun pick out chestnut streaks in her dark glossy hair and his eyes wandered up and down her frame, from the creamy skin of her neck to the trim waist and hips that moved from side to side as she walked. Thinking himself to be a very pious man he had long ago eschewed the desires of the flesh but this was so hard! He usually dealt with middle aged matrons or old crones, women more like Biddy Shaw, and this girl had awoken feelings in him that he had long ago forgotten – he wanted her and oh so badly!

When they reached the village the vicar's wife, Mrs Sudbury, was nervously waiting for them. "I thought it best to do this kind of thing in the church – maybe safer for us."

"Just so madam; now you know what you are looking for – any disfigurements, marks that look out of the norm, third nipples, extra digits – anything that worries you, and if you find anything, wherever it is, you must call out immediately, this is no time for false modesty, this is The Lord's work." He turned to John Evans, "You and I John will take up position by the main door just in case and," he turned to Jenna and her examiner "I suggest you go into the vestry where it is a little more private." Earlier he had noticed that Biddy had a mole beside her nose and one behind her ear so, as if he'd had an afterthought he addressed Mrs Sudbury, "I suppose we should let Mrs Shaw accompany you – in fact as she is so sure we have a Witch in our midst, I would like you to examine her too in order that you can compare good with evil."

Biddy Shaw was invited in looking like the cat that had stolen the cream - that is until she realised that she too was under scrutiny. "But this ain't regular – I mean, I'm no witch."

Story Telling Seventeen

Josiah put a reassuring hand on the woman's shoulder "Of course you're not my dear, and everyone knows it, so you have nothing to fear." He ushered the three women into the vestry and closed the door. After a while they heard raised voices, it was difficult to distinguish the words but Biddy Shaw's voice was unmistakable. Sometime later a worried looking Mrs Sudbury appeared and beckoned to the two men who asked in unison, "Well? Does she show any signs?"

"Well yes and no." Josiah's heart sank. "What do you mean woman, does she have any indications or does she not."

"Well the girl, no, but I think you should come and look at this." When they entered the room both women were still in their shifts. Jenna blushed and lowered her eyes but Biddy, who was clutching her shift tightly around her glared at the two men.

Mrs Sudbury nodded towards the older woman "She has a large lump under her breast, I'm not sure if it is a nipple but..." Biddy shouted out, she was scared now, this was terrifying, "It's but a mole that's all. I weren't born with it; it just came up without me noticing. There's nothing wrong in that, now let that be an end to it and..." Josiah was much relieved that Jenna was safe and cut the older woman off in full flow. "We will have to make a judgement now sister, if you would be so kind as to let us take a look." Biddy started to protest but the much practised pair held her firm and parting her shift they lifted her left breast revealing a large black mole that could, if so desired, be misconstrued as a nipple. Josiah thought that actually it may be some form of malignancy but he exclaimed for all to hear "Oh dear Lord, this surely is a nipple to feed the devil's spawn! Get the witch away from me." Shocked to the core, Biddy screamed out protesting her innocence but he struck her hard across the face. "Go and tell the villagers this evil creature has been found out. She'll hang for sure and it can't be done soon enough for my liking."

Biddy was dragged off still dressed only in her shift and protesting her innocence loudly, but so afraid was everyone of meeting the same fate that no-one went to her aid or comforted her. She was eventually given back her clothes before being locked in her own barn until a trial could be arranged.

The next morning Jenna called on Mr Shaw. He was a broken man – torn between what he knew to be the truth; that his wife may be a spiteful vindictive woman but she was not a witch, or of speaking up for her for fear of being a marked man, guilty by association. Jenna persuaded him to allow her to visit poor Biddy and he was touched by her compassion, especially under the circumstances. Ashamed and afraid of his wife now and not wanting to confront her, he removed the latch that held the door firm and Jenna slipped in.

It was dark in the barn with just the odd shaft of sunlight piercing through the gloom. Biddy knew who her visitor was – she had sort of been expecting her. Jenna knelt down so that she and Biddy were face to face. In the gloom Biddy became aware of a quiet rustling, of movement. She felt Jenna take her hand and begin to stroke it and then something brushed her face. As she peered into the gloom Jenna moved into a shaft of sunlight so that Biddy could see her clearly and what she saw made her freeze in horror. The girl's eyes were round in shape now and amber in colour with one dark vertical slit in the centre. Biddy sat rigid with fear, unable to move as a forked tongue stroked her face. Oh dear God! She was looking into the face of the devil and she had never been so afraid.

A moment passed and Jenna moved, concealed once more by the shadows. Biddy was aware of the soft rustling again and as the creature opened the door to leave she saw that it was once more in human form.

"Have a nice hanging Biddy, I'll come to watch, it's the least I can do." She slipped out from the barn locking the door firmly behind her, smiling to herself as she listened to Biddy's screams and warnings that the devil himself was amongst them. Poor Biddy!

Josiah Adams had tossed and turned throughout the night. Thoughts of the girl tormented him. Maybe when they had finished here he could persuade her to leave with him, or maybe he could settle in the village as her husband. He walked out of his lodgings stretching himself in the sunshine and thanked the Lord that he had followed his instincts. That dear sweet girl was no more a witch than he was and as for the old hag, well maybe it was time she got what she deserved.

What is health and wellness?
© Sarah Dawkins RN, BSc (Hons), MSc, AMC. 2019

Health and wellness is not just about the lack of disease, it is an active process. We cannot expect to be healthy without conscious thought and actions. We have to make choices and take action to be healthy, it doesn't happen on its own.

There are many dimensions to health and wellness; Emotional, Physical, Spiritual, Intellectual, Occupational, Environmental, Social, Financial, Sexual and Recreational.

1. **Emotional wellness** is a priceless commodity. We spend many hours doing things we believe will make us feel happy. Emotional wellness has many factors.

Self-Care - Is about loving and caring for yourself. Are you attentive to your thoughts, feelings, behaviours and emotions in order to learn, accept and grow from the situations you find yourself in?

Self Esteem – Is your own judgement of your worth or abilities and is about respecting yourself. How do you value yourself?

Self-Compassion – Is about extending compassion to yourself in times of perceived inadequacy, failure, or general suffering. Do you give yourself the same care you would give to others in their time of need?

Void – Some people have an emotional void and look outwardly, filling it with drugs, alcohol, food, relationships, or material possessions. Is this you?

How do you deal with your emotions?

2. **Physical wellness** is what people generally think about when we talk about health and wellness.

Story Telling Seventeen

Personal Responsibility – Is required in all aspects of your life that are necessary to keep yourself in top condition.

Activity - Is about expending energy through bodily movement. It doesn't require a gym membership, there are plenty of things you can do to get your body moving. What do you do to stay active?

Nutrition – Comes from a well-balanced diet and will allow you to function at your best. This involves eating a rainbow of coloured fresh foods every day. What do you eat?

Rest - Is important for repairing, refreshing and rejuvenating your immune system and body. Do you get enough sleep or rest? Are you physically well?

3. **Spiritual wellness** involves being in tune with your spiritual self and balancing your inner needs.

Peace and Harmony – Is it established in your life?

Life - Do you understand the meaning of your life and can you appreciate how your life experiences and events can define your purpose. Are you congruent with your values and actions as you live your life?

Faith - Spiritual wellness can be defined by your faith, values, ethics and morals. The path to spiritual wellness can involve meditation, prayer, affirmations or spiritual practice to support your connection to a higher power or belief. It doesn't have to be about religion, although it can be if you choose.

Compassion - The capacity for love and forgiveness, altruism, joy and fulfilment will help you engage in your spiritual wellness to find harmony between that which lies within and the social and physical forces that are on the outside.

Are you in tune with your spiritual wellness?

4. **Intellectual wellness** is the ability to open your mind to new ideas and experiences.

Active participation – Do you actively participate in expanding your mind, are you creative and do you undertake mentally stimulating activities to expand your knowledge and skills? Do you assimilate what you learn with your life experiences?

Problem solving – Do you explore issues related to problem solving, creativity and learning? How do you solve problems? Do you share them with others, take time out to think about them? Or bury your head in the sand?

Creativity – Do you value and nurture creativity? Are you curious and undertake lifelong learning and exploration?

Are you intellectually well?

5. **Occupational wellness** is the ability to achieve a balance between your work and leisure time.

Career Goals - Your working life encompasses much of your time. Do you love what you do? And have you set yourself career goals?

Attitude – What is your attitude to work? Have you explored your career?

Opportunities – Have you pursued all the opportunities that come your way?

Stress - Have you identified your work stress and conflict so that you can deal with it effectively?

How are you with your occupational wellness?

6. **Environmental wellness** is all about recognising your responsibility of being respectful of your surroundings to promote a healthy environment.

Story Telling Seventeen

Harmony – Do you live in harmony with the Earth by understanding the impact of your interactions with nature and your personal environment?

Behaviours - You can become environmentally conscious by understanding your behaviours and practices, leading a lifestyle that is respectful of the environment to minimise any harm.

Outdoors – Do you spend time outdoors and enjoy the natural beauty of the world around you?

How do you rate your environmental wellness?

7. **Social wellness** is concerned with developing assertive skills and being comfortable with yourself.

Relationships and Interactions – How are your relationships and interactions with friends, family and others in your world?

Healthy Boundaries – Have you created healthy boundaries, meaningful relationships, respect for yourself and others as well as creating support systems that include family and friends?

Emotional resilience – Do you undertake active listening to help you to build emotional resilience and empathy?

Reflect on your social wellness. How well are you, socially?

8. **Financial wellness** involves seeking to improve and maintain your financial situation.

Expenses – Have you learnt how to successfully manage your finances?

Habits – Do you have smart habits to maximise your financial wellness and reduce your stress?

Strategies – Are you proactive and seek strategies to build financial wellness, like paying off any loans, keeping accurate financial records and looking for and negotiating discounts.

Story Telling Seventeen

Plan ahead - Are you balanced in your spending. This will assist you to become financially well. However, it is a process and won't happen immediately.

A lack of financial wellness can lead to a loss of productivity and engagement. How financially well are you?

9. **Sexual wellness** is the state of physical, emotional, mental and social well-being related to sexuality; it is not merely about sex or the absence of disease, dysfunction and infirmity.

Intimacy – Is there any within your relationship(s)?

Love - Is defined as a measure of selfless give and take, and acts as a major facilitator of interpersonal relationships.

Body Image - Encompasses what you feel, see and believe about your own body. Feeling ashamed, self-conscious or anxious will reduce your desire for love and intimacy.

Honesty -The freedom to be honest within your relationship has the power to build trust and create love and intimacy. How honest are you?

Through sexual wellness and love, we gain an emotional connection. This helps form the basis of a great relationship How do you rate your sexual wellness?

10. **Recreational Wellness** includes a broad range of leisure activities and represents a rewarding form of human experience.

Leisure - Is defined as the productive, creative, or contemplative use of free time and can be spent alone or with others. What do you do with your leisure time?

Relaxation - Many people take part in recreation, as a form of relaxation from the pressures of work and other tensions.

Story Telling Seventeen

Creativity – It allows you to express creativity, expose hidden talents, and pursue excellence in various forms of personal expression.

Release - Active recreation can offer a channel for releasing hostility and aggression.

How do you rate your recreational wellness?

Health and wellness starts with you. Are you conscious of your lifestyle choices? Do you need to make any changes to achieve your full potential?

I wish you health, wellness and happiness in your life.

© Sarah Dawkins RN, BSc (Hons), MSc, AMC. 2019

**

Eating Out

For the greatest lovers
of fine food, eating out
will always be such a joy.
Whether tackling salad,
soup or peppered steak
make no mistake this lad
will relish it with pleasure,
treasure every last slice
of cake, and take his time
finishing a glass of wine,
lingering long with glee
over an Irish coffee.

Richard Seal

Ada's Law
By Trudie Oakley

A charming yarn of policemen on the job another episode will appear in Story Telling eighteen.

November 25th 8.30pm

Inspector Nick Murray put down the phone "We've got another one Josh."

Sergeant Josh McGiven looked quizzically at his superior "Another what Gov?"

Another body; one shot to the body and one to the head and I'm guessing the bullets will be 22 calibre just like the others. Someone called it in from the Shedwell Estate and our local lad was on the scene almost immediately – reckons this one can't have been dead more than an hour."

Josh leant back in his chair with his hands behind his head, "That makes six in the last nine months and we've got no idea who's doing it, or why! They look like gang related executions but so far none of the victims fit that kind of picture." He grabbed his jacket from the back of his seat, "Typical, it's pissing down and we've got to get soaked because there's some maniac roaming around like pretending to be John Wayne."

"You could have something there Josh. Maybe there is some crazy vigilante out there punishing these men, but for the life of me I can't see any connection between them – maybe this one will give us a clue."

Story Telling Seventeen

Two weeks earlier

The Shedwell Estate was a run-down collection of miserable looking concrete monoliths that housed what society tended to call 'problem families' and that looked more like a prison camp than a housing estate.   The roads surrounding it had been narrowed by concrete blocks in order to stop joy riding and speed humps proliferated.   The one good thing in its favour was that it was surrounded by fields and common ground and was therefore a popular spot for joggers and dog walkers.

Ada walked Bobby there quite regularly and on this particular November afternoon as she was returning to her car, she heard raised voices and then a woman screaming.   As she was putting her key in the lock a woman came running towards her sobbing and clutching her head and not being able to see through her tears, she collided with Ada. It looked to Ada as though she had been punched on the nose, and pretty hard at that as one of her eyes was beginning to swell.   She was sobbing uncontrollably and shivering violently. Her coat was undone and Ada could see that she had scant clothing underneath it – she obviously left home in a hurry.

"Whatever is the matter my dear? You'll catch your death out here dressed like that." She unlocked her car, "Here, come on sit inside with me for a while. I'll start the engine and get the heater going."   The young woman did not resist and let Ada guide her into the passenger seat. Ada grabbed Bobby's rug from the back seat and wrapped it around her, "Now who did this to you – can I take you to the police station?"

"No, no. I'll be alright. You're very kind – whatever must you think of me I..."

"I'm thinking that somebody has hit you and," she'd noticed the marks on the woman's arms, "I'm guessing that it's not for the first time."

"He doesn't mean it. I just annoy him. He's lovely really – he's just frustrated 'cos he can't get a job and....."

"I know, I know, it's not his fault it's yours."

The woman began to sob again, "I'd better go back – my little boy will wonder where I've gone. He'll be frightened." She pushed down the rug and began to fasten her coat.

"Why do you stay with him?"

The woman wiped her eyes on the handkerchief that Ada had offered, "Because I love him."

Ada sighed and shook her head "They all say that."

A rough looking man appeared and started walking purposefully toward them. At the sight of him the woman started and opened the car door, fear written all over her face, "I've got to go but thank you."

"Wait, what's your name?"

"Julie, it's Julie. Please go – he doesn't like me talking to people," and with that she was off.

Ada watched as the couple met and the man put his arm around his woman, ruffling her hair. She started the car and looked at Bobby in the rear view mirror, "It's all honkey dory now, eh Bobby – until the next time that is."

On her regular walks with Bobby Ada kept an eye out for Julie but although there were plenty of young women pushing tots in prams none of them were her. A couple of weeks went by and one afternoon on a whim she called into the local supermarket on her way home from dog walking and virtually bumped into her. If anything Julie looked worse than before. Her swollen eye had receded but her top lip was badly swollen, and her arm was in a sling. "Hello dear. Oh my, what happened to you?" Julie made a half-hearted excuse about falling down but they both knew the truth behind her injuries.

"Why don't you let me buy you a coffee dear and ..."

"No, no. I've got to go, he doesn't like me being too long. He's waiting in the car park. See you sometime," and with that she was gone.

....

As Ada sat by the fire that evening sipping her port and lemon she pondered on the ways of the world. Her mind drifted back to her own childhood and her own unbending cruel father who had ruled his little kingdom with a rod of iron, beating her mother up whenever he was 'in a temper'. As a consequence Ada and her younger brother Sid had left home at the earliest opportunity. They both regretted leaving their mother with such a brutal man, but although they tried hard to persuade her she would not leave him and had unselfishly encouraged them to get away and 'make their way in the world'.

She had enlisted in the WRACS at the earliest opportunity and her career in the army had taken her to places where she had witnessed the abysmal lives that so many women in the world were subjected to. She had developed an abiding hatred of the cruelty and injustice meted out to them by men just because they could. It had struck a chord with her, reviving memories that she had tried so hard to forget and reinforcing her conviction that men were not to be trusted and to be avoided where possible.

Consequently, she was well beyond the first flush of youth when she'd met Stan. He was a career soldier whose first wife, not being suited to army life, had divorced him. The friendship that had developed from the occasional social meetings had caught them both by surprise and after several months they had to admit that they were in love. They were married and had nearly twenty seven blissful years together before Stan lost his battle with illness leaving Ada alone and inconsolable. She sipped her port and stroked Bobby's head as she remembered those dreadful days so thankful of the dog's existence.

She thought back to the day that Stan had come home with the Beretta. The situation around their posting abroad had become uncertain and things seemed to be taking a turn for the worse. Stan dismissed any questions she had as to how he had obtained the gun, only saying that he was worried about her safety and he'd got it 'just in case'. That night she had been given a tutorial on how to take it apart, load and clean it and the next day he had taken her to a deserted area to show her how to use it.

Eventually they had retired to the terraced house in the leafy suburb in which she still lived, and the gun had come with them. Occasionally Stan would take it out to clean and oil it and understanding her feminism and knowing how strongly she felt about men who abused their position Stan had often joked about her using it. "There you are Ada. If anyone gets on your nerves just get 'em down a blind alley and pop 'em off – tell 'em you're administering Ada's Law."

She poured another drink and sighed deeply. He'd laughed at his joke – she wondered what he would think about her now.

November 25th 6.00pm

Ada turned off the gas under her stew, told Bobby to be a good boy while she was out and, after checking for the umpteenth time that her auburn wig and loaded Beretta were in her shopping bag, drove off her forecourt into light traffic. It was a chilly night but not as cold as it could be in November and she was glad of that. She stopped a couple of streets away and pulled on her wig, making minor adjustments in her rear view mirror and once satisfied she drove off once more. Her eventual destination was the Shedwell Estate but she chose to park a good ten minutes walk away close to a large block of flats on the basis that it was a busy thoroughfare and neither she nor her car would be likely to lodge in anyone's memory. She fitted her crook lock then began to make her way to the vantage point she had chosen.

She knew from earlier observations that her target was in the habit of spending most of his evening in The Queens Head, and she knew that rather than walk along the streets, he preferred to take the short cut across rough ground that separated the estate from his watering hole. She nestled as best she could into the small group of gorse bushes near the entrance to the rough path and waited hoping that he would appear. She was getting too old to be standing around in the cold and of course there was always the possibility that he would choose to stay in the warm himself.

The main entrance to the Estate was well lit so she had a good view of anyone entering or leaving. She must have been waiting for at least half an hour, although it felt much longer and she was just about to give up and go home, when she spotted a man walking in her direction. As he passed under one of the street lights her heart skipped a beat – it was him!

She took off her gloves and reached into her bag taking out the gun and slipping it into her coat pocket. She looked all around and listened but there seemed to be no-one else about. When her quarry was a few metres away she stepped onto the path and feigned distress. "Oh please help me. I seem to have lost my way," she made up a name, "I'm looking for Queens Road – do know it?"

The man peered into the gloom annoyed with the silly old bat, "Never 'eard of it. Go and ask a police."

But before he could finish his sentence Ada took the gun from her pocket, aimed and fired hitting her target square in the chest as she told him "This is for Julie." As he lay on the ground she bent over him and shot him once more in the head. "Belt and braces Ada – belt and braces." Heart thumping she stood still listening hard - all was quiet thank The Lord. Slipping the gun back into her bag she retraced her steps trying not to hurry, listening all the while for chasing footsteps.

Once back in her car she felt a little safer. Her hands were trembling which made it hard to deal with the crook lock so she forced herself to just sit back and listen to the radio for ten minutes until she had regained some control. The last thing she wanted was to be involved in some sort of accident. Gradually she calmed down and was able to release the lock on the wheel. She switched on the wipers to clear the screen as it had now begun to rain and after a few more minutes she set off for home.

She began to relax as she neared her house and slipped off the wig as she drove and a few minutes later she was thankful to be pulling onto her forecourt safe and sound. She pushed her car door to hoping that none of her neighbours had noticed her brief absence then let herself in where she received a rapturous greeting from Bobby. Once all was calm she hid the bag containing the gun and wig in her secret place and made her way into the kitchen.

"Now then Bobby let's see about something to eat shall we?" She heated up the stew she'd made earlier and prepared Bobby's dinner. She ladled the steaming stew into one bowl for her and put it on a tray alongside the dog's bowl then carried it into her lounge where she placed it onto a nest of tables that sat beside her favourite armchair. "There we are then Bobby", she put his bowl down onto his feeding mat then picked up the television remote as she plumped up cushions, settled into her seat and placed the tray on her lap. "Now, let's enjoy our meals and see if there's anything worth watching on the tele."

....

November 25th 11.45pm

Josh sat in the now empty office listening to the rain that was lashing hard against the windows. It hadn't taken long to ascertain the identity of the victim or where he lived. He always hated having to break the dread news of a death to families but in this instance the man's partner, although shocked, did not seem exactly heartbroken to hear of his demise, in fact Josh thought he detected a sense of relief. It was obvious that she had been used as a punch bag and it crossed his mind that maybe she had arranged the murder, but he instantly dismissed the idea – she was patently a victim and probably always would be; the likes of her just didn't take control - their lives were always run by someone else.

It was late and he should have been home ages ago, but these cases were getting to him. His desk was covered with the files of the other five men seemingly gunned down at random. He leant back in his chair running his hands through his hair. Six murders now and apparently nothing to tie the victims together, and no witnesses other than one elderly lady out walking her dog who said she had heard shots and had been the first to reach the body of the first of the victims. She'd seen a man running away in the distance but couldn't help with a description as her eye sight wasn't up to much, but she thought he must be young as he seemed to run very fast – the only witness statement they had and it was as much use as a chocolate fireguard.

He gathered up the paperwork leaving it in a neat pile on his desk – he'd have another look in the morning with a fresh head. He left the office switching off the lights as he closed the door; bid farewell to the night duty officer and hurried out to his car with his jacket draped over his head. Bloody rain!

**

21 Rules For
a Good Old Age

Some of us have reached our golden years, and some of us have not.

But these suggestions should be read by everyone. They have been collected from many a senior, each with his or her own piece of advice. Some you know, some may surprise you, and some will remind you of what's important. So read well, share with your loved ones, and have a great day and a great life!

Story Telling Seventeen

1. **It's time to use the money you saved up. Use it and enjoy it.** Don't just keep it for those who may have no notion of the sacrifices you made to get it. Remember there is nothing more dangerous than a son or daughter-in-law with big ideas for your hard earned capital. Warning: This is also a bad time for an investment, even if it seems wonderful or fool-proof. They only bring problems and worries and this is a time for you to enjoy some peace and quiet.

2. **Stop worrying about the financial situation of your children and grandchildren**, and don't feel bad spending your money on yourself. You've taken care of them for many years, and you've taught them what you could. You gave them an education, food, shelter and support. The responsibility is now theirs to earn their own money.

3. **Keep a healthy life, without great physical effort**. Do moderate exercise (like walking every day), eat well and get your sleep. It's easy to become sick, and it gets harder to remain healthy. That is why you need to keep yourself in good shape and be aware of your medical and physical needs. Keep in touch with your doctor, get tested even when you're feeling well. Stay informed.

4. **Always buy the best, most beautiful items for your significant other.** The key goal is to enjoy your money with your partner. One day one of you will miss the other, and the money will not provide any comfort then, enjoy it together.

5. **Don't stress over the little things**. You've already overcome so much in your life. You have good memories and bad ones, but the important thing is the present. Don't let the past drag you down and don't let the future frighten you. Feel good in the now. Small issues will soon be forgotten.

6. **Regardless of age, always keep love alive**. Love your partner, love life, love your family, love your neighbour and remember: "A man is not old as long as he has intelligence and affection."

7. **Be proud, both inside and out**. Don't stop going to your hair salon or barber, do your nails, go to the dermatologist and the dentist, keep your perfumes and creams well stocked. When you are well-maintained on the outside, it seeps in, making you feel proud and strong.

8. Don't lose sight of fashion trends for your age, but **keep your own sense of style**. There's nothing worse than an older person trying to wear the current fashion among youngsters. You've developed your own sense of what looks good on you - keep it and be proud of it. It's part of who you are.

9. **ALWAYS stay up-to-date**. Read newspapers, watch the news. Go online and read what people are saying. Make sure you have an active email account and try to use some of those social networks. You'll be surprised which old friends you'll meet. Keeping in touch with

what is going on and with the people you know is important at any age.

10. **Respect the younger generation and their opinions**. They may not have the same ideals as you, but they are the future, and will take the world in their direction. Give advice, not criticism, and try to remind them of yesterday's wisdom that still applies today.

11. **Never use the phrase: "In my time".** Your time is now. As long as you're alive, you are part of this time. You may have been younger, but you are still you now, having fun and enjoying life.

12. Some people embrace their golden years, while others become bitter and surly. Life is too short to waste your days on the latter. **Spend your time with positive, cheerful people**, it'll rub off on you and your days will seem that much better. Spending your time with bitter people will make you older and harder to be around.

13. Do not surrender to the temptation of living with your children or grandchildren (if you have a financial choice, that is). Sure, being surrounded by family sounds great, but **we all need our privacy**. They need theirs and you need yours. If you've lost your partner (our deepest condolences), then find a person to move in with you and help out. Even then, do so only if you feel you really need the help or do not want to live alone.

14. **Don't abandon your hobbies**. If you don't have any, make new ones. You can travel, hike, cook, read, dance. You can adopt a cat or a dog, grow a garden, play cards, mahjong, checkers, chess, dominoes, golf. You can paint,

volunteer at an NGO or just collect certain items. Find something you like and spend some real time having fun with it.

15. Even if you don't feel like it, try to **accept invitations**. Baptisms, graduations, birthdays, weddings, conferences. Try to go. Get out of the house, meet people you haven't seen in a while, experience something new (or something old). But don't get upset when you're not invited. Some events are limited by resources, and not everyone can be hosted. The important thing is to leave the house from time to time. Go to museums, go walk through a field. Get out there.

16. **Be a conversationalist**. Talk less and listen more. Some people go on and on about the past, not caring if their listeners are really interested. That's a great way of reducing their desire to speak with you. Listen first and answer questions, but don't go off into long stories unless asked to. Speak in courteous tones and try not to complain or criticize too much unless you really need to. Try to accept situations as they are. Everyone is going through the same things, and people have a low tolerance for hearing complaints. Always find some good things to say as well.

17. Pain and discomfort go hand in hand with getting older. **Try not to dwell on them but accept them as a part of the cycle of life** we're all going through. Try to minimize them in your mind. They are not who you are, they are something that life added to you. If they become your entire focus, you lose sight of the person you used to be.

18. If you've been offended by someone - forgive them. If you've offended someone - apologize. Don't drag around resentment with you. It only serves to make you sad and bitter. It doesn't matter who was right. Someone once said: "Holding a grudge is like taking poison and expecting the other person to die." Don't take that poison. **Forgive, forget and move on with your life**.

19. If you have a strong belief, savour it. But don't waste your time trying to convince others. They will make their own choices no matter what you tell them, and it will only bring you frustration. **Live your faith and set an example**. Live true to your beliefs and let that memory sway them.

20. Laugh. **Laugh A LOT**. Laugh at everything. Remember, you are one of the lucky ones. You managed to have a life, a long one. Many never get to this age, never get to experience a full life. But you did. So what's not to laugh about? Find the humour in your situation.

21. **Take no notice of what others say about you and even less notice of what they might be thinking**. They'll do it anyway, and you should have pride in yourself and what you've achieved. Let them talk and don't worry. They have no idea about your history, your memories and the life you've lived so far. There's still much to be written, so get busy writing and don't waste time thinking about what others might think. Now is the time to be at rest, at peace and as happy as you can be!

AND REMEMBER: "Life is too short to drink bad wine."

A Precautionary Tale

Graham Strachan

I've been unable to get to the computer since Sunday due to an unfortunate incident with the local wildlife.

Living in the mountains of Murcia, we can come to meet a variety of wildlife. Wild boar freely roam but are rarely seen. It's more likely, in the event of a rainy period, you may see evidence of their existence in a family of footprints where they've been drinking from a puddle. If you do see them, it's worth giving them a wide berth, just in case, as the Mothers can be very protective of their young, emphasis on the word "Wild".

Then there's the birds of prey, which are various and comparatively numerous. We are fortunate to have a wide variety of Eagles in particular, with the greatest one being the magnificent Golden Eagle. There are scorpions, snakes, lizards and all sorts of other critters, most of which keep a respectful distance and we all live harmoniously.

Yet there is one form of wildlife which spreads fear amongst the population due to the voracity of its weapon. It is with this ferocious beast that I met with my unfortunate incident at the weekend. I speak of course of the.........**Processionary Caterpillar!**

"What", I hear you shout derisively, "A Caterpillar, you're kidding?" If only I were.

Story Telling Seventeen

I don't know about other parts of the world but this Caterpillar is widespread in Spain wherever there are Pine trees.

There is massive publicity, particularly at certain times of the year, that warn the public about the dangers of being in close proximity to these deceptive creatures.

I say deceptive because I think of my childhood in London. We lived on a street that had trees down both sides of the road at about twenty metre distances (it'd have been measured in yards then). In those days in the 60's when we weren't a pesticide driven society I could probably find up to twenty different varieties of caterpillar close by. Smooth, hairy, long, short, green and brown, to suggest only a few types. In fact they were my pals and I would often play with them (I even made a caterpillar hotel at one time, but that's another story). The point of my reminiscing is to explain that to me caterpillars could do no harm. Then, as an adult, I moved to Spain and on Sunday I found out how wrong my premise had been.

So, back to the current "Precautionary Tale".

As I said, since moving to Spain twelve years ago I have been well aware of the danger of these larval insects. The main cause for concern though is not a human one but actually a canine one. If a dog should come into contact with one of these creatures it will likely be dead within five minutes if it doesn't receive immediate medical treatment.

They create nests in Pine trees (They're called "Sacs" for obvious reasons, see pic). This year, due to a mild winter to date, they were slightly earlier than normal as it is more often to be February before they begin to show their existence.

At a certain time of year, dependant partially upon the climate, the caterpillars release from the sac and feed on their host pine tree. Once they have had their fill of that tree they go on the move in search of another one. They are also migrating to find a suitable area to burrow and become cocoons in their next stage of development.

We had noticed a few sacs in the two pine trees on our land, something which had never been evident in our previous six years at the house.

I cut down all but one sac removing them far afield away from people. The final one was so high up in the tree, the branches of which overhang an edge, it was impossible for me to remove it. By the way, the advice is never to deal with these things yourself and certainly don't cut them down but, hey ho, what do they know?

Amazingly, I got away with this action. In fairness to me I should say that the Spanish authorities are well known for 'sledge hammer and nut' scenarios so a lot of advice is often treated with a pinch of salt.

Moving on to last Sunday. My wife and I, and one of the dogs, were in the outer garden. The other three dogs were, fortunately, on the other gated side of the garden. My wife looks down and says, "Oh my God, look!"

There at her feet was a long line of Processionary Caterpillars!

They follow the leader nose to tail in order to make sure the group stay together. There is a myth that they follow in this manner because they are blind, which doesn't really make sense unless there happens to be a 'chosen one' that has the ability of sight. In fact they give off a scent from their rear end (Don't we all) and that is why they travel in this way

A quick removal of Frida, the aforementioned dog, and then we both sprang into action. Bucket of boiling water, protective clothing, including three pairs of gloves.

Gingerly, keeping the assassins at arm's length, we collected them and dropped them into the bucket, which was laced with our homemade concoction of vinegar soup. Whilst I was away disposing of the resultant stew, and warning a close neighbour, Naomi was disinfecting the area as best as she could. I returned and we did a pace by pace search of the garden to look for any further evidence of the caterpillar's presence. Thankfully, as far as we could tell, there were no others.

Move the clock forward thirty minutes and I start to itch on my neck, another thirty minutes I'm now in considerable discomfort. The itching is due to large lumps on my neck and lower face. As each minute passes the symptoms become more extreme. My head is on fire and my eyes are weeping. That's the time we realise we're out of "Piriton" the anti-histamine drug. A quick trip to a local friend and we borrow some from them. I took the dosage but it didn't have any significant effect.

Naomi, as is her normal practice, then went into research mode and learnt all she could about the creature, which had caused such a virulent reaction in me. It turned out that we had been working on a slight misapprehension. We were aware the problem was due to the toxicity of something within the hairs of the caterpillar. What we didn't realise was that this didn't relate to the visible hairs on it's body. In fact there are microscopic hair-like tubes filled with the toxin. They are so small apparently that they may pass through, all but specifically designed protective, clothing. My pain was testament to this fact. Once in direct contact with the skin these tubes release the toxin into your body. I guess an added complication during my attempt at removing the dastardly foes was, whilst not blowing a gale, there was a fair wind blowing which clearly assisted the unseen enemy to do its worst.

The afternoon and evening continue with an ever increasing burning, itchy rash. I tried to have an early night, but sleep largely eluded me as the pain and irritation was so intense.

I arose the next morning, in as much pain as I had been the previous night. I could barely leave my face alone. I went to the bathroom to poor cold water over my face, an action that I've repeated frequently since. I glanced up at the mirror and was shocked by what I saw. A quick cancellation of my morning's work and a trip to the health centre for shots and medication ensued.

Today, the swelling, irritation and pain has receded enough to allow me to write this piece. I'm not out of the woods yet, my eyes are streaming and I'm still wanting to scratch the incessant itchiness but, by comparison, I am far better than I was.

I've left the photo of yesterday's beautiful visage till last. Prepare yourself....it's not a pretty sight.

So, my precautionary tale is here for you to be warned if you should ever meet these guys yourself....phone NASA or some such agency.

I usually look better than this.........honest!

**

Horizons

Richard Seal

The sea has always held an enduring allure for Gerry. He grew up in a rural part of the West Midlands, which felt like such a long way from the seaside, so the annual family summer holiday trip to Weston-Super-Mare was an extra special treat for him. He looked forward to it for months. On arrival in the town, the first thing that the lad wanted to do was to change into his swimming costume and get straight down to the shore. He was not particularly interested in spending his free time in amusement arcades, sunbathing; playing with a Frisbee or making sandcastles, his overwhelming desire was to surrender himself to the sea at the earliest possible opportunity.

Standing on this familiar beach now, watching his two boys playing football nearby, takes Gerry back thirty years to the fun-filled hours that he spent here with his older brother Will, who played such an instrumental role in fostering his love of the ocean:

"Come on, Gerry, let's go in the water now, the waves look great!"

"But it's very windy at the moment, Will, and look - the red flag is flying."

"You know what that means don't you?" The older boy grinned. "The sea is extra exciting when the flag is flapping - the red does not mean danger, it stands for daring, adventure and fun!"

The two of them loved nothing more than to be knocked off their feet by the breakers, and then dragged under the churning surf, only to emerge laughing hysterically and spitting out salty mouthfuls. Gerry found that he was also thrilled by the feeling of struggling to stand up as his little legs were almost pulled out from under him by the powerful current, the cloudy water sucking the gritty, swirling sand, stones and shells.

The boys could not wait to take their new inflatable boat out onto the open sea. Will was quick to reassure his brother that he knew exactly what he was doing.

"Don't worry, we will be fine, and we won't go out too far anyway."

Gerry was enjoying the ride, but felt a little concerned that their vessel was moving so quickly. "Will, can you slow it down a bit, we're going very fast?"

Story Telling Seventeen

"It's okay, everything is under control. You'll be safe with me."

The younger boy noticed that they had strayed into a darker area. "Why has the colour of the water changed? And look, there are little ripples on the surface now, instead of waves."

Will was unwavering in his positivity, as ever. "This is called a rip tide, I have read about them. It's nothing for us to worry about though, we just need to stay calm and we will be out of it in a minute."

Just seconds later, the boat capsized, and the brothers were immediately submerged in the surge. When they reached the surface, Gerry found that his strength was already stalling, his limbs felt leaden, almost deadened by the shock and exertion.

"Hold on tight, Gerry, it's not a problem, honestly, these things just happen sometimes. We will be rescued soon."

Clinging limply to the deflated boat, awaiting his fate as the beach receded, Gerry was filled with curiosity and awe rather than being gripped by panic and fear. He managed to stay calm, and felt sure that he would be safe in the company of his big brother, although he barely managed to hang on until help arrived.

Having survived the ordeal by dinghy, and been on the end of severe reprimands from mum and dad, the indefatigable Will then became fixated by his grandest scheme - for the two of them to be the first people to succeed in swimming all the way to the horizon. The boy was adamant that this would be achievable.

"We'll be famous, Gerry, just wait and see. Think about all the autographs you'll be asked to give. No-one has done it before - I'd love to see the horizon up close."

"Are you sure about this, Will, it seems such a long way away?"

"It won't be hard for strong swimmers like us! Besides, we will be able to rest on a desert island or two on the way, and see if we can find Robinson Crusoe."

"Really, do you think he might be there?"

"Yes, why not? If he isn't we can always set up our own desert island home. We would be able to survive in the wild, just like him and his friend Friday."

"But what about food?"

"Oh there will be lots of fresh fruit there and fish to catch, things like that. It will be such fun. No fast food for you for a while though, I'm afraid." He nudged the younger boy playfully, and gave him a wink. "Cheeseburgers don't grow on trees, you know."

As they started swimming, Gerry could feel the adrenaline rush, but after a few minutes he started to find it hard going. "I feel tired already, Will, I don't think I will be able to do it. Can we have a break yet?"

His brother sounded rather breathless. "Stick with me, stay close, we will be there soon I'm sure."

Gerry could not help thinking that their target seemed to be moving further away rather than closer, steadily retreating towards far-off lands. The waves suddenly seemed to be getting bigger and bigger, and he could no longer feel the sand beneath his feet. "Will, what's happening? It's so deep," he gasped. Panic was starting to rise.

"I know. Hang on, I'll swim back towards you... "

To this day, Gerry is not clear about what happened next. He remembers coughing and spluttering as he floundered, then everything went black. He was later told that he had been incredibly lucky to have been saved, and he realised that ambition had outstripped the boys' strength and senses. Not surprisingly, the tragic incident proved to be the final straw for his parents, who decided that all future family holidays would be city breaks. Looking out at the horizon again, the man smiles as he dwells on the beloved older brother who never returned that day, knowing that he must have reached the elusive pale blue line.

Cochin International Airport

Tucked down in the toe of India serving the area of Kochin is the first green airport to be built in the world. It was constructed under a private and public ownership and work started on the structure in February 2014, the facility opened for travellers in March 2017, and during the period of operation has handled 62,000 movements of aircraft.

There are two passenger terminals one for International flights and another for Domestic Travellers and the facility can handle all types of modern aircraft including the latest wide bodied jets and those giants with two storeys.

The airport is unique in that it is totally reliant on its own power supply, which came on line in the later part of 2015, comprising of a Solar Plant generating 48 megawatts of electricity per day. There are 46,150 solar panels laid out over 45 acres of land close to the facility. So that the land is not lost to farming all types of vegetation is grown beneath the panels to ensure maximum use of the land.

Healing

Story Telling Seventeen

Richard Seal

Everything had seemed so different to Eric after Sally died. He was continuing to sit on the sofa watching the same television screen in the unchanged living room, where his wife's slippers were still beside her chair, but the frequency of life had changed, it had been subtly re-tuned to create a strange place with an alien face. They had had an enduring marriage, with unspoken love and intermittent laughter and joy.

Janet, Eric's daughter, has lived nearby for a couple of years, and she had been a great strength and support since Sally's final, protracted battle with the ravages of cancer. The middle-aged woman juggles her job in a shop with family life and keeping an eye on her father, bringing him an evening meal. Initially numb to everything, and unable to do anything more than go through the motions, acceptance was now starting to descend upon the bereaved man.

Eric had never really wanted anything for himself, he had spent eight decades trying to provide for his wife and daughters, preferring to listen and react to other people's stories rather than creating his own. The man was now starting to stay in bed for longer and longer, finding some sanctuary hiding away beneath the sheets. The more concern his daughter expressed about his welfare, the more lethargic and listless he seemed to become.

The day that Marky arrived, Eric's pilot light showed signs of flickering back into life. An elderly neighbour had passed away leaving her twelve year old cat without a home, and Janet had volunteered her father into looking after him until something else could be arranged. Initially the old man felt anxious that he no longer had the ability or inclination to take care of himself, let alone an animal. His daughter reassured him that the cat would be good company, and not to worry.

The afternoon after his arrival, Marky padded up to the old man's bedroom. As he lay in limbo with his eyes closed, Eric could hear the light drilling sound and sensed it calming his nerves. He tentatively stretched out his hand, and it settled gently on the cat's back. Marky responded by deepening his purring and flexing his paws. As the vibration filled him with a relaxed energy, Eric drifted between sleep and a meditative state.

As each day starts with Marky's arrival and ends with him curled up at the end of the bed, existence seems more positive, and Eric spends more and more time living in the moment with his healing companion. Janet seems very happy to see them together too. The man feels free to appreciate just being, not speaking, and while he has no fears about the prospect of death, he now hopes that it does not arrive any time soon for him and his new friend.

**

Architectural Designer.

To Remove a Wall

It was a beautiful summer's day when I drove down into Somerset from my office in Bristol following up an enquiry where somebody wanted to improve the size of their home. On arrival at the address, from a lane beside the house in question, three vans that sold ice cream were leaving in convoy.

The front door of the place was open, although I called there was no answer. I walked through into a property that was in disarray. Some of the internal non-supporting walls had been removed. In the backyard I could see a man with his face under the bonnet of another ice cream van. There was another man standing to one side who I discovered was the driver of the vehicle which would not start.

Finally, after the engine of the van spluttered into life and the driver drove the machine away, my new client turned his attention to me. We walked up to the house and he wanted it to be enlarged with a two storey extension to the side covering the small lane which turned out to be access to the rear of his property.

The house was an ex council dwelling on the end of a terrace built in the nineteen twenties. He had been making changes to the inside and after a visit from a Building Inspector, no doubt who had been informed by one of the neighbours of what was happening to the property, he was told he needed planning approval especially as he had changed the use of the property from private to commercial.

He was a lively person, a little shorter than me, always doing something and talking saying what his plans were in the ice cream industry. To talk to him and receive instructions was a little difficult. Although in the end I understood he wanted the living room to be as large as possible and en suites in each of the bedrooms. Being an old Council House it was large but I thought to myself not that large for what he wanted. Following the survey I left him ... it was like a breath of fresh air being away from him and the energy my new client conveyed.

Story Telling Seventeen

Sometimes Planning Departments surprise me, despite my warning to him that it was doubtful that we would get the change of use from private to commercial past the Authority, it went through without question.

On looking further into the site I was able to confirm what he had told me that there was a rear access to the property, which had been hidden from view whilst I was there by a row of worn out sheds.

I drew up the plans extending the house to the section over the side access. Fitting en suites to each bedroom was not possible because of drainage and a space situation. However, I made use of what was available and all in all I was happy with what had been achieved and I drove back down to present them to him.

He did not take much interest in the drawings and accepted them without fuss. I had the feeling the written word was a little difficult for him to understand. As far as I was concerned I had achieved what he required, a set of drawings which had been presented to the Local Authority and were passed by the Planning Office and the Building Inspector.

Story Telling Seventeen

A few months went by before I received a call from the Inspector asking to meet him on site, which was unusual. When I arrived the house was still standing but only just as my client had taken a quantity of the end wall out so as to enlarge the living area into what was the side lane. As I said I don't think he understood what the blue prints were telling him.

The Inspector put up signs to say the building was dangerous and was not to be entered into and wound yellow tape round the openings to discourage access. Although I am sure when the Inspector and I left the client ignored all those ribbons and went into the property, in his mind he must have been wondering where else he was going to live.

We finally managed to rescue the situation. As I had instructed Chris, a qualified Structural Engineer who we frequently worked with, and after a few visits to the site the property was made secure.

**

Quotation from Hitler
"Great Liars are also great magicians."

Taking Hold

Richard Seal

It was one of those July afternoons when the light seemed to be extra bright, emanating from somewhere else somehow, and the colours of everything around her appeared more vivid. On such a lazy hazy day, Alice could not help but wonder why it was necessary to be at school. The lower sixth form internal exams were over, and everyone knew that the next year was the really significant one. The dying days of this summer term just felt like marking time.

At lunchtime she decided to give her classmates the slip and spend some time doing some reading and possibly write a little poetry. Alice was half way through 'The Great Gatsby', and was totally enraptured by it. She had not told her friends about her writing, doubting that they would be very interested. In fact, she did not particularly like any of the girls, and could not care less about parties, clothes and shoes. Moreover, her feelings about love and relationships were too personal to be shared with them.

Story Telling Seventeen

Alice wandered down to the far corner of the playing fields, beyond the reach of football games and any chattering huddles, and found a cool spot in the shade of a huge oak tree. She put 'Gatsby' in her lap for a moment and gazed out over the fields beyond the low fence: were they looking back at her, just as they had done to countless wistful teenagers over the centuries? The girl luxuriated in the thought, aware that an idea was taking hold in her consciousness.

She removed a single sheet of folded blank paper from between the leaves of her book. The girl breathed deeply in anticipation of losing herself in another world, feeling the magic as the poem runs away with itself, and is no longer in her control. By the end of that hour Alice had resolved to always find time for things which enrich existence and nourish the spirit. She felt sure Gatsby would approve.

**

"I have come to the conclusion that politics are too serious a matter to be left to politicians. "
Charles de Gaulle

**

Ice and a Slice

Richard Seal
Does it matter how many?
No-one is keeping count
or judging her on amount
she consumes every night
just as long as she avoids
starting a fight and keeps
drinking quietly - her crying
is no concern of the staff ..
The barmen are quite nice,
calm, professional, offering
the ladies ice and a slice ...

*"We learn from experience that men
never learn anything from experience."*
George Bernard Shaw

And Finally ... A man was looking for a place to sit in a crowded university library. *He asked a girl: "Do you mind if I sit beside you?*

The girl replied, in a loud voice "NO, I DON'T WANT TO SPEND THE NIGHT WITH YOU!"

Story Telling Seventeen

All the people in the library started staring at the man, who was deeply embarrassed and moved to another table.

After a couple of minutes, the girl walked quietly to the man's table and said with a laugh: "I study psychology, and I know what a man is thinking; I bet you felt embarrassed, right?"

The man responded in a loud voice:"$500 FOR ONE NIGHT? ..... I`M NOT PAYING YOU THAT MUCH!"

All the people in the library looked at the girl in shock.

The man whispered to her: "I study law, and I know how to screw people".

Percychatteybooks
Story Telling (R)
Somerset House
6070 Birmingham Business Park
Birmingham
B37 7BF
Registered Number 2299335